Bone Treasure

In a sheltered basin, high up in Colorado's remote Rocky Mountains, two field collectors discover an awesome array of dinosaur bones. Knowing that two competing and irreconcilably hostile palaeontologists will pay big money for knowledge of such a find, the men realize that they have struck *bone treasure*. Unfortunately for all concerned, a supposedly extinct race of Anasazi Indians regards these relics as sacred and is prepared to slaughter anyone who tries to remove them.

Only one of the men makes it back to Denver, his hair turned prematurely white by his horrifying experiences – but what he brings with him sets off an unstoppable chain of events.

Joe Eagle, a frontiersman desperately in need of money, agrees to lead a large party into the Rockies to plunder the fossil beds – but word of the find has got around and their ruthless competitors are never far away. And somewhere up ahead, the terrifying Anasazi await them all. . . .

Bone Treasure

Paul Bedford

A Black Horse Western

ROBERT HALE

ISBN 978-0-7198-2503-3

The Crowood Press
The Stable Block
Crowood Lane
Ramsbury
Marlborough
Wiltshire SN8 2HR

www.bhwesterns.com

Robert Hale is an imprint
of The Crowood Press

Typeset by
Derek Doyle & Associates, Shaw Heath
Printed and bound in Great Britain by
CPI Group (UK) Ltd, Croydon, CR0 4YY

To Stephen G. Compton, with grateful thanks for your original suggestion for this story

CHAPTER ONE

No amount of imagination or speculation could have prepared them for what lay ahead. With the magnificent snow-covered mountain known as Pike's Peak looming to the south, Joe Leidy and Ben Mudge had plenty of natural beauty to behold, and yet it all counted for nought. Because, as they wearily led their horses down into the natural basin formed in the Colorado Rockies, an even more breathtaking sight awaited them.

All those vague rumours and whispered stories had turned out to be true after all. Bleached glistening white, after apparently spending aeons under the relentless sunshine, an awesome collection of bones was strewn around on the hard ground. But what made these relics so special was their sheer size and rarity. They had never belonged to the skeleton of a mere human, or indeed any *living* creature currently known to mankind. The remains of a buffalo or even a massive grizzly were nothing by comparison.

'Sweet Jesus, we've actually gone and done it,' Joe

mumbled, his tired eyes wide as saucers as he peered incredulously around. 'Found everything we was sent out for, and then some! We don't even have to dig 'em up. It's like treasure for the taking.'

Surprisingly, Ben was more restrained. Not because he wasn't excited, because he sure as hell was – it wasn't every day that someone tripped over such a huge horde of dinosaur bones. It was just that something about them puzzled him as well. Gratefully coming to a halt, he dropped to his haunches and groaned. That last stretch through the high country had been gruelling beyond belief. And as a dizzying climax to the journey, they had just crossed a deep ravine by way of a narrow rock bridge that unbelievably seemed to defy gravity.

It was difficult to accept that civilization in the form of Denver, Colorado, was a mere eighty miles away to the north-east. Under normal conditions that sort of distance would mean two days' ride, but there was nothing normal about travel in the Rocky Mountains. For the last seven days they had been clambering ever higher, and it had taken its toll. The air was undoubtedly thinner and every task was harder . . . even thinking. And so it was only after thoroughly scratching his bearded chin that Ben finally replied.

'Don't you think there's something mighty odd about both the positioning and condition of these bones? It's not as though they've been spat out by earth movements or some such. It's almost like they've been *arranged* in a certain way. And look, there's not even any earth or rock fragments clinging to them. You could say they're on display.'

His companion glanced at him in disbelief. 'You've had too much sun, *hombre*. This ain't Main Street, Denver, with a storekeeper arranging his pegs and flat irons for sale. And in any case, I ain't clapped eyes on another living soul for days. Just accept it, we've struck it lucky. Huzzah!'

Ben stared at him long and hard, until finally he reluctantly nodded agreement. The sun had only just past its zenith, and it really was powerful hot. 'Happen you're right. Reckon I'm just tired and hungry, is all. Let's get a fire going before we start looking these bones over. If they've been here for millions of years, they sure as hell can wait until we've rested and eaten.'

As Ben and Joe wolfed down their food, the deliciously savoury smell of bacon and beans wafted over their small campsite, shortly to be followed by the unmistakable odour of coffee. Even in such a remote region, they had had little trouble in obtaining ample firewood. Limber pine trees grew up to eleven thousand feet above sea level, clinging to rocky outcrops of the kind surrounding the basin. Shaped by the wind, they were gnarled and twisted, but their wood burned well. It did not occur to either of the jubilant collectors that they had just made a huge mistake.

'God damn, but them was fine vittles,' Joe announced, topping his remark off with a massive belch.

9

Ben, his mouth still full, nodded his whole-hearted agreement. The two men were sitting on blankets, with their backs to a large rock near the edge of the basin. That desolate piece of land stretched away for some few hundred yards before them, literally littered with bones. Their two horses and one pack mule were hobbled nearby.

'I vote that we make an inventory of what's here and sort out a few prime specimens to take back with us. And then we spend the night here,' Joe continued. 'We've earned a rest and *Mister* Marsh will just have to cool his heels in Denver for a while longer. What that impatient son of a bitch doesn't know, won't hurt him . . . or us!'

The other man, having finally finished eating, was settling a coffee pot on a small tripod over the fire. 'Sounds hunkey dorey to me,' he responded with genuine enthusiasm. His earlier anxiety had subsided along with his hunger, but even so, something was still niggling him. 'While this coffee's heating up, just take a look-see at the layout of those bones. Please!'

Joe sighed, but did as he was requested. Although this was their first expedition together, he had developed a real liking for his bearded companion, and so didn't want to offend him. Contentedly patting his full belly, he sauntered over to the nearest array. The first specimen that he looked at was all of three feet long and six inches in diameter! And that was nothing compared to some of them. The sheer scale of their find took his breath away. And yet . . . as he gazed around at their stupendous discovery, a slight chill descended on him. There was something odd about the positioning of them. A certain symmetry that couldn't possibly have occurred naturally. And then there was the fact that they were completely pristine, with no detritus whatsoever attached.

Turning back to the fire, he noticed that Ben was staring intently at him. 'OK,' Joe called back. 'So maybe someone *has* been here and tampered with them, but that doesn't mean it happened yesterday, for Christ's sake. These things were lying around long before creatures like us even got to shuffling around.'

Ben's mouth opened to reply, but he never got the words out. Instead, as though by some exquisitely malevolent timing, an unearthly noise echoed around the hillside behind their camp. It sounded like a type of horn and yet there was an eerie quality to it that cloaked both men with unease. Even their animals were unsettled, pawing the ground and straining against their hobbles.

It was Joe that spoke first. 'What the hell was that?'

His companion swiftly scanned the surrounding hills. Not a soul was visible. 'Maybe it was just the wind.'

'What wind?'

Ben turned to face him. There had been no repeat of the sound, but anxiety was etched across his normally placid features. 'I think we should take up a few of those damn bones and leave, now!'

Joe glanced up at the sun and then shook his head

emphatically. 'We spent too long lolling around in front of that fire. It'll take us a while to get organized and I ain't stumbling around in those hills in darkness.'

The other man brooded on that for a while before finally nodding agreement. 'I guess you've got the right of it. But if we *are* passing the night here, then I want a big fire. If there's a mountain lion or some such beast out there stalking us, flames might keep it away. And let's have the packs all made up so that we can load up and move out at first light.'

Neither man cared to pursue the notion of how any four-legged predator could possibly have created the sound they had just heard.

As the last of the light ebbed out of the sky, the landscape took on a whole new appearance. The surrounding hills were distinguishable only by their darker hues, and shadows produced by the blazing fire danced around the campsite. Yet unlike previous nights, these seemed only to create a sense of menace rather than contentment, a feeling experienced by both men. Taking up his military issue Springfield carbine, Ben released the 'trapdoor' over the breech and inspected the seating of the 45/55 cartridge for perhaps the fourth time.

'I hadn't given it much thought before tonight, but I kind of wish Marsh had laid out on something more modern, like Winchesters.'

Joe grunted expressively. 'Huh, he'll have got

these things cheap, through some contact in Washington.'

In truth, the Springfield was a sturdy, reliable weapon, but the need to reload after each shot meant that its rate of fire was far slower than the latest repeaters. None of which would have mattered on a simple palaeontological expedition, except that both members of it were feeling unaccountably jittery. Still, they had finished their work without any further distractions, and the mule had been loaded with a varied selection of bones. Ben had even picked out a particularly impressive specimen and fastened it to his saddle-bags . . . just in case. And now, they had nothing more to do until daylight. With the fire built up and spare wood ready nearby, they settled down to sleep. The only problem was that neither of them could relax.

'What was that?' Joe muttered nervously as he squirmed around on his blanket. His earlier scepticism had completely disappeared with the light, and now he found himself wishing that they had taken their chances in the hills.

'What was what?' Ben responded testily. 'All I can hear is the fire crackling and your heart thumping.' Then a stone shifted somewhere above them and he instinctively reached for his carbine.

Before either of them could say anything else, sounds of movement came from various points beyond the range of the firelight. Both men recognized their fatal positioning at once. A large fire highlighted them to anyone or anything, whilst

13

severely affecting their own night vision.

It was the bearded collector who reacted first. 'I reckon we've maybe got a big cat prowling around up there. It's smelt our food and now it wants us. Let's get our gear around the other side of the fire, so that it's between us and the rocks.'

Joe glanced at him, nodded, and then clambered eagerly to his feet. Yet before he could actually do anything, a piercing shriek erupted from the hillside and instinctively he turned around to face it. By so doing, he perfectly presented his torso to receive the stone-headed spear that flew out of the darkness. The vicious projectile slammed deep into his chest and sent him staggering back towards the flames.

Momentarily ignoring his stricken companion, Ben had the presence of mind to retaliate. Cocking his Springfield, he aimed at a vague shape on the hillside and fired. More by luck than good marksmanship, his bullet obviously struck something, because it resulted in a great howl of agony that seemed to collectively grow until the frightening wail was coming from all sides.

Desperately trying to control the terror that threatened to overwhelm him, he flicked open the 'trapdoor', automatically ejecting the empty cartridge. With trembling fingers, he rammed in a fresh one and then turned to take a look at his companion. The unfortunate collector had collapsed painfully close to the fire, his front drenched with blood. Ben grabbed his jacket and heaved him back, so that the flames were between them and their mysterious assailants.

One glance at the dreadful wound was enough. The crudely fashioned spearhead had penetrated with tremendous force, so that it was literally embedded in Joe's chest. Its removal was out of the question, and the injury was clearly fatal. Although almost out of his mind with pain, the dying man somehow managed to grab Ben's arm.

'They've kilt me, Ben. Ride out while you can!'

That man stared at him in horror, barely able to comprehend such a request. Then he glanced up at the hillside and his stomach churned. A score or more of apparently human forms had become dimly visible in the flickering light. They seemed to be covered in some form of dust or chalk that gave them a sinister, amorphous appearance. Then one of them launched a rock towards the intruders – which was, of course, how the two collectors were perceived.

Ben fired at the nearest form and watched it fall back spurting blood. So at least they *were* human and could be killed! But that was little consolation when faced with so many. A volley of rocks flew towards the fire. Unable to dodge them all, he was struck solidly on the left shoulder, whilst another gashed his forehead. Joe cried out with renewed agony. Lying helpless on the ground, he had been hit many times.

Fumbling with his breechloader, Ben finally got another cartridge in, but he knew that no amount of them would be enough. Turning to his stricken companion, the dreadful realization came to him that flight was the only option. Tormented by guilt, he called out, 'I can't do nothing for you, Joe.'

The other man nodded grimly. Blood frothed from between his lips and out of his nose. His strength was failing fast, but somehow he made a superhuman effort and drew his Colt revolver. His intention was obvious. With studied determination, he spat out four words. 'Ride . . like . . . the . . . devil!'

As the strange apparitions began to close in on the campsite, Ben ran for the animals. With no time to spare, he sliced through all the hobbles with his hunting knife and then mounted his horse. Yelling like a banshee, he kicked the frightened beast into motion. Already desperate to flee, it needed no other urging and raced off across the basin. Joe's horse and the mule followed on, but the fugitive had scant interest in them. Personal survival was now all that mattered.

As they careered over and through the bone formations, a communal howl of anger erupted behind them, followed by six rapid gunshots. Then there was a short silence, broken by a high-pitched scream that seemed to last forever. Ben knew that that could only be his doomed companion. Guilt over his own survival would surely follow, but for the present his only concern was to stay alive. With so many bones spread around, the going was treacherous – and suddenly the inevitable happened.

From close behind him there came a great clatter, followed by high-pitched whinnying. Joe's horse had tripped, but Ben wasn't about to turn back. Then, ahead of him, he could just about make out the basin petering out into rougher ground.

Knowing that he had put some distance between himself and the camp, he slowed down. There was little point in breaking his neck, because if those infernal creatures were also ahead of him, then he was finished anyway.

Deliberately resisting the temptation to glance back at the fire, he utilized his improving night vision to help his horse clamber up the hillside. He wasn't really certain of the way, but he knew that nothing could induce him to return over the narrow rock bridge. As a lone fugitive, he would just have to force his own trail back down to civilization, even if it took far longer.

The sheer horror of the night's events clung to him like a shroud. His survival was so terribly uncertain, and yet growing inside of him was a steely determination to make it back to Denver. If nothing else, Joe deserved a Christian burial, and since their ambitious employer was bound to come after the bone treasure, there would likely have to be a reckoning with the creatures that took his life!

CHAPTER TWO

Joe Eagle could remember a time when Denver had been just a collection of grubby tents pitched next to the South Platte River – but this was no longer. Ahead of him, on the grandly named 17th Street, lay the Brown Palace Hotel. A large, two-storey building, it was a sign of changing times. After a number of devastating fires, more and more public buildings were being constructed out of brick, and this was a prime example. Impressively solid and luxurious, it served as a good advertisement for the city's growing prosperity.

Unfortunately, *some* things never altered. After hitching his horse to the solidly constructed rail outside the hotel, the broad-shouldered visitor entered the lobby and gazed around at the amazing opulence. Sadly he was given little time to appreciate it, because within a few seconds a suited flunky had bustled officiously round the desk, his hand raised to bar the newcomer's path. As the man peered suspiciously at him, Joe sighed with annoyance. He knew exactly what was coming. It was also a fact that if he hadn't been unnecessarily distracted, he would undoubtedly have sensed the close scrutiny that he had come under from a 'hard case' lounging near the entrance.

'No dogs and no Indians allowed in here,' came the familiar affront. 'If you're looking for a place to sleep, try the livery. I'm told the straw is changed regularly, ha ha.'

Joe's heart began to beat slightly more quickly, and he could feel his jaw tightening. As a dangerous glint came into his eyes, the man before him suddenly regretted his hasty words: he had just noticed the huge knife held in a sheath on the Indian's belt, and tales of lurid atrocities leapt into his mind. Others in the lobby paused to watch the outcome with detached interest, because of course they weren't under threat. But then abruptly, the whole strained atmosphere was transformed.

From one of the downstairs rooms, a burly bearded individual in an expensively tailored frock-coat appeared. 'What's happening here?' he boomed out. 'Why are you obstructing my guest?'

The flunky's eyes widened like saucers and he gratefully stepped back. 'My apologies, Mister Marsh. I had no idea!'

'Well, now you *do* have an idea,' the man snapped back, then completely ignored him. Thrusting his hand out, he continued, 'You must be Joe Eagle. I've heard a lot about you, and all of it good. Come with me, please. We have much to discuss.'

Before Joe even had time to respond, he found himself ushered into a private dining room containing three other men. Their appearance could not have been more different. One seemed to be a mere 'city slicker' in a store-bought suit, whilst the next quite obviously lived on the frontier: he wore well-used range clothes and a holstered six-gun strapped around his waist. But it was the third man who really claimed Joe's attention. Probably in his mid-thirties, his hair and full beard had turned prematurely white, and there was a recent scar on his forehead. As their eyes momentarily met, Joe could almost feel the anguish in them. It occurred to him that such angst could well have a connection to his own presence in the room.

Surprisingly, considering Marsh's obvious enthusiasm to proceed, it was the rough-looking character who spoke first, and what he had to say didn't bode well for the meeting's prospects: 'I'm gonna have to have words with the owners of this place. I didn't think a hotel like this would let some *'breed* just wander in off the street! And what the hell kind of name is Joe Eagle, anyhu?'

As on so many occasions before, Joe felt cold rage flow through his lean body. He had long ago learned how to control his emotions when faced with an all-too-familiar insult – and this one was obviously vicious and calculated to wound, unlike the casual invective from the desk clerk. His immediate reaction was to walk slowly over to his abuser until they were almost face to face. With eyes like chips of ice,

20

he took in the weathered features of the fellow before him.

'You run your mouth kind of reckless, mister. But for what it's worth, I'm actually one eighth Cherokee. If that means anything to a lily-livered shit-head like you!'

What happened next was something that he would never have predicted. Instead of retaliating either verbally or physically, the other man momentarily favoured him with a hard stare, before suddenly breaking into a broad grin that totally transformed his features.

'He'll do for me, Mister Marsh,' he loudly remarked to their host, who had obviously deliberately remained by the door. Then he slowly and carefully proffered his right hand to the man that he had just insulted. 'No hard feelings, Joe. I just needed to get your measure, is all. It counts for a lot when you're riding with a man.'

Joe regarded him coolly for a moment before accepting the firm grip. 'I reckon I can see the need for that. Just don't make a habit of it, yeah?'

With that settled, Marsh swept in to take charge of the proceedings. 'You've just met Dave Cartwright. Now let me introduce you to the others.'

Joe had been on the point of moving on, but that name pinned him to the spot. 'Buckskin Dave?'

'The very same,' that man responded affably. 'Although I'll allow I don't wear them very often nowadays. They don't take to rain so well.'

For the first time Joe smiled. 'Well, I've certainly

heard of you.'

Keen to continue, Marsh waved towards the individual in a suit. 'This is my assistant, Tom Hayden from the Peabody Museum of Natural History at Yale.'

Joe Eagle was abruptly out of his depth. 'The what from where?'

Marsh smiled indulgently. 'I know this is a lot to take in Mister Eagle, but we are both palaeontologists. That means we collect fossils . . . bones of creatures that are extinct, such as dinosaurs. Very definitely dinosaurs.' He paused momentarily as he noticed the other man's confusion. 'In other words, huge animals no longer living. We are very shortly to commence an expedition into the Rockies in search of just such things, and on the advice of Mister Cartwright here, I want you to join us.'

Joe was totally mystified. 'I think you must have got the wrong man. I don't know anything about bone collecting.'

Marsh briefly glanced at Cartwright before answering that. 'Let me introduce you to Ben Mudge. I believe that when you've heard what he has to say, you'll understand why we need you. And I think we'd all be better off seated, because even now it's not easy listening.'

It was quite some time before Ben Mudge, quietly spoken and very intense, finally finished his harrowing tale. After he had concluded with the story of his tortuous escape back to civilisation, all four

spectators sat in silence for some moments. Even
Marsh seemed temporarily lost for words, although
he had obviously heard it all before. Joe had listened carefully to every word. He had observed the
effort that it took Mudge to recount the terrible
events and he had no doubt that it was all true . . .
or at least that man's interpretation of it.

'Have you ever fought Indians before, Mister
Mudge?'

'No, never.'

Joe nodded thoughtfully. 'Well it seems to me like
you just have. Although I'll allow that they don't
sound like any tribe I've ever heard of. One thing's
for sure, Mister Marsh, it ain't just the terrain you
need to worry about.'

Tom Hayden spoke up for the first time. 'Sounds
to me like you could be running scared!'

Cartwright glanced at the assistant and snorted
contemptuously, but left it to Joe to respond.

'Yeah, the thought of fighting Indians again does
scare me. Any man says it doesn't is a damn liar. And
if you didn't have shit for brains, you wouldn't talk
like that.'

Hayden coloured angrily, but before he could
react, Marsh motioned for him to remain silent. It
was obvious to him that Joe, who had returned his
attention to Ben Mudge, had plenty more to say.

'You say they killed your partner with some kind of
spear. Did you hear any gunshots at all?'

'Only my own and Joe's.'

'That's very unusual, what with all the Indian

traders about, and government treaty *presents*. But even if they had no firearms before, they've sure as hell got your partner's now.'

Ben's response to that was puzzling. 'I don't reckon those bastards will know how to use them.'

Marsh couldn't restrain himself any longer. 'What the devil do you mean by that?'

Fresh anguish came to Ben's features, as he relived the raw memories. 'Only that the spear they murdered Joe with had a *stone* head, and they were hurling rocks at us. I don't think they possess anything made of metal. Which must mean they've never had contact with white men before.'

Marsh was astounded. 'Don't be absurd. It's 1877, for God's sake!' Nevertheless he glanced at Joe for confirmation.

That man appeared to be deep in thought, but in reality he hadn't missed a thing. 'Maybe, maybe not. If they've always stayed up in the high country, they *could* have avoided contact ... although I admit it's unlikely. But one thing is for sure, if they've laid claim to these bones and know every inch of the terrain, they could be very dangerous indeed.'

Marsh nodded his head contemplatively. 'That's why you're here, Mister Eagle.'

'You want me to risk my life for a pile of bones?'

'No, you'll be risking it for the pile of money that I'll be paying you to protect me. And from what I hear, you possess a great hunger for money!'

Joe's eyes narrowed, but he chose not to pursue that last statement. Instead, he gestured towards

'Buckskin' Dave. 'If everything I've heard about this man is true, you don't really need me.'

Cartwright shook his head decisively. 'All my life I've followed the frontier as it's moved west. I know the land and its people, but I'm still not one of them like you are. And where we're headed, I reckon we'll need that difference.'

That was all the confirmation that Marsh needed. Eagerly seizing Joe's hand, he announced, 'Mister Eagle, there's the find of the century awaiting me up in those mountains. You're hired!'

Joe nodded his acceptance, but he also had something else to say. 'I have to tell you I feel sad for whoever is living up there.'

'Why so?' his new employer queried.

'Because if by some miracle they *have* avoided contact with the white man, they won't be proof against any of his diseases. Whether they choose to fight or not, us going up there to bring back the bones of dead creatures will probably mean the end of them as well!'

Although known as something of a 'penny pincher', it transpired that Othniel Charles Marsh actually had access to a great deal of money, even though that hadn't always been the case. He had inherited a fortune from his uncle, George Peabody, and was now determined to utilize it to further his scientific reputation and that of his family's museum. To that end, he had parted with a sizeable wedge of cash at the local stock barn and now owned a large string of pack mules. Since it was intended that these beasts should transport the recovered bones out of the mountains, Joe decided to check them over. But as he approached the stables where the animals had been taken, two bruisers made their move.

They came from opposite sides of the street, their movements obviously pre-planned, as though they were cutting out a steer. Joe spotted them in plenty of time and slowed to a halt, his hand over the butt of his holstered revolver. Both men were clad in store-bought suits similar to Tom Hayden's, and rather incongruous bowler hats, but they possessed hard, mean eyes and were quite obviously not scientists. Their Remington revolvers were carried in holsters worn high on their hips, to enable a quick draw. Since they kept their hands studiously clear of their weapons, Joe merely stood his ground and waited.

It was the one on the right who had the words: 'I've been told to offer you ten dollars to step over to my boss's railroad carriage.'

'And it took the two of you to deliver that message, yeah?'

The 'hard case' tilted his head slightly, as though trying to decide whether that had been a statement or a question. 'We always work together, 'cause some folks don't always take to us.'

Joe nodded. 'I can understand that. So where's this carriage?'

The one on the left gestured vaguely across town and muttered, 'Not far.'

Joe grunted. 'And the ten dollars?'

'When we get there.'

Joe chuckled mirthlessly. 'That figures. OK, let's go. You two both in front, where I can see you.'

The three men headed north a short distance. There were actually four rudimentary stations in Denver, each linked to a separate railroad company, and they arrived at the one that served the Denver Pacific Railroad. A highly polished carriage sat in splendid isolation on a siding. Joe regarded it pensively for a moment. He really didn't know what he was letting himself in for, but then again, that had never stopped him in the past. And then, of course, there *was* the ten dollars.

Following the two hired guns over to the carriage, he grabbed the handrail and clambered up the steps on to the open-air platform. The door opened before him and curiosity did the rest. He entered a world of highly polished luxury that reminded him of the hotel, and was greeted by a tall gent standing, or rather posing, behind a mahogany desk. The man was clad in an expensive frockcoat that greatly resembled the one worn by Joe's new employer. But there the similarities ended. This individual had a lean frame and boasted a full head of hair along with a luxuriant moustache that continued on down below his chin. A sharply protruding jaw line gave him an aggressive air, which was soon to be confirmed by his speech.

'My name is Cope. Edward Drinker Cope,' he announced, as though it should definitely mean

27

something. Looking his guest carefully up and down, he continued with, 'I have recently been notified that you are the man that I need to help with my expedition into the Rocky Mountains.'

Joe kept his tone even. 'Well if you know that, it's likely you also know that I've already got a job. Besides, seems to me that the man you really need is a fellow called Ben Mudge. He knows exactly where to find the bones, which is more than I do.'

Cope grunted. 'I would have to agree with you on that, but sadly Mudge seems to feel some misplaced loyalty to his portly employee. He doesn't seem to realize that Marsh is just a moderately gifted amateur. If he goes wandering up into the Rockies, he'll come to grief just like that poor fellow that worked for him. You have my word on that.'

'You seem to be very well informed.'

'I make it my business to be. You see, I represent the Academy of Natural Sciences in Philadelphia. It is my intention that they will benefit from that massive *and* priceless horde of dinosaur bones, not some tin-pot museum funded by Marsh's dead uncle.'

It occurred to Joe that Cope had maybe said a little too much. 'How would you know so much about those bones unless you've had men up there yourself?'

The other man shrugged dismissively. 'There's more than one way to skin a cat, Mister Eagle. But enough of this. You start immediately. I want to be ready to move as soon as they do.'

'You seem to be very sure that I want to work for you.'

Cope snorted as though the alternative hadn't occurred to him. 'Oh, you'll jump ship all right, *Joe Eagle*. You need money and I'll beat anything that Marsh is paying you.'

'Which means that you already know how much that is.'

Cope frowned with annoyance. 'Don't try to be clever. It doesn't suit you. Oh, and when next we meet, you'll address me as *Mister* Cope.' He gestured to one of his men. 'Show this . . . *gentleman* where he sleeps. I have more important business to attend to.'

Meeting abruptly over, the two assistants turned to follow Joe out of the carriage, but he was far from finished. 'I done told you I'd got a job with Mister Marsh, and I intend to keep it. Apart from anything else, I don't reckon you and I would knit together too well.'

Cope appeared bewildered, as though his mind had genuinely been on other matters. 'Just what are you saying?'

'What I'm *saying*, is you can stick your job where the sun don't shine. But before I go, I want the ten dollars that this man of yours promised me.'

Cope's jaw seemed to jut out even further as he absorbed the calculated insult. 'I don't think I like your attitude, Eagle,' he retorted, and then to his men. 'Throw him out!'

The two men were professionals and they enjoyed their work, but they hadn't expected such a sudden turn of events. Joe, on the other hand, had deliberately antagonised their employer, knowing full well what would happen. So he was ready, and he always fought to win. Grabbing the nearest chair, he swung it in a vicious arc before him, so that the polished wood connected solidly with both men. As they fell back under the violent assault, Joe could easily have slipped out and left . . . but that wasn't his way. Besides, he was owed money and fully intended to collect.

After casually hurling the chair at Cope's startled features, he pivoted to his left and kicked out at an unprotected midriff. His victim expelled air in a great whoosh and Joe followed it up with a smashing blow to the man's nose that sent him tumbling back across his boss's desk, howling in pain.

Perversely, it was Cope who then quite likely saved his life by barking out, 'No shooting!'

Joe twisted to his right to find the other thug impotently holding a revolver, his confusion plain to see. Instinctively, he launched himself across the carriage, brushing the weapon aside and forcing his opponent back into the nearest window. The rear of that man's head shattered the glass, sending shards of it crashing to the trackside. Joe brought his right knee up again and again, so that his adversary doubled over in pain. Seizing the helpless individual's jacket, he then swung him around and hurled him bodily into the carriage door.

The hapless thug crashed through glass and timber on to the open platform, falling sideways down the steps. There were startled cries outside, but Joe ignored those and instead turned to face the livid fossil collector.

'Ten dollars!'

Completely disregarding the anguished groans of his other stricken employee, Cope reached into a pocket and reluctantly extracted a single gleaming Gold Eagle coin. Placing it on the now scratched mahogany desk, he disdainfully slid it over. His anger was plain to see, but even so, the coincidently humorous side of the situation hadn't entirely escaped him.

'An Eagle for an Eagle, eh? Well, you'd better enjoy it while you can, because you will come to regret this day's work. We won't always be in a relatively civilized town.'

As his fingers closed over the ten-dollar coin, Joe favoured the older man with an icy smile. 'The frontier is my home. When you leave here, it is you that needs to beware. *And* I've learnt something from this little shindig. For an ass-wipe like you to be involved, those old bones really must be worth a shit-load of money. I didn't believe that until now.' With that, he abruptly turned away and cautiously shouldered his way through the wrecked door. The scene that met his eyes brought a broad smile to his bronzed features.

At the side of the track, 'Buckskin' Dave Cartwright, also with a beaming grin on his face, stood with his revolver covering Cope's battered thug. That man had just got to his knees, and now watched in weary resignation as Joe descended the steps.

31

'I guess you must have been following me.'

'You guess right,' Cartwright agreed. 'We thought Cope might make a play for you. What we didn't know was how you'd react.'

'And now you do.'

'Oh, yeah. And so do they.' Without warning, the older man reversed the grip on his Colt and brought the butt down solidly on to his prisoner's skull. The luckless fellow toppled forwards into the dust without a sound. 'I reckon we've outstayed our welcome here.' So saying, he backed off, followed by a grateful Joe Eagle. A number of Cope's staff, drawn by the disturbance, watched them depart, but no one made any attempt to stop them.

Once they were out of sight of the carriage, Cartwright holstered his gun and glanced meaning-fully at his companion. 'You know what all this means, don't you? We ain't just got a band of unknown hostiles to worry about. There'll also be those sons of bitches dogging our trail.'

Joe chuckled. 'Seems like it's a good thing you've got me on your payroll then, don't it?'

CHAPTER THREE

Two days after Joe's 'interview' with Edward Drinker Cope, and with first light barely registering, a lengthy file of men and animals quietly wended its way out of Denver. Marsh's intention was that they should be gone before anyone realized it, but his latest employee knew that no interested party would be hoodwinked for long.

As they left the city limits behind them, Joe looked down the length of the column. There were ten riders in total. In addition to the five principal members of the expedition, another five men had been hired as teamsters to control the mule train of twenty animals. That many creatures on the move meant plenty of revealing dust, which was another reason why such an early start hadn't really been necessary.

Taking Ben Mudge's dire warning to heart, Marsh had reluctantly purchased ten of the latest Winchester 1876 Model carbines. With 22 inch barrels, the heavier framed weapons fired 45/75 car-

tridges, making them easily manoeuvrable man-stoppers and more robust than earlier models. Joe had
gratefully accepted the powerful repeater, but knew
that in a close-up fight the sawn-off shotgun hanging
from his saddle horn would likely prove more effec-
tive.

Their aim was to follow the course of the South
Platte river up into the high ground for as long as
possible. This important source of water was formed
way up in the Rockies by the confluence of the South
Fork and Middle Fork. It would keep the expedition
supplied, as they slowly made their way up through
the foothills from Denver and on into the steep-sided
Platte Canyon that truly marked the start of mountain country.

Since the beginning of the journey was the only
occasion when the going would be considered easy,
the expedition's scout decided it was time to get
under Ben Mudge's skin a little. To that end, he
urged his horse forward and came up alongside him.
As that man glanced over, Joe smiled amiably.

'I'm guessing that your hair wasn't white until that
last trip.'

Mudge recoiled slightly, as though taken aback by
such directness. He wasn't given chance to reply.

'Only it puzzles me why you should agree to return
after what you went through. I'm asking because
there's things I need to know, if we're all to stay safe.'

The field collector pondered for a long moment,
as he tried to decide whether to open up to a com-
parative stranger. Then the stark reality of what they

were likely to face together made up his mind.

'I didn't know Joe Leidy long enough to call him "friend", but he was my companion on that fated quest and I left him to die at the hands of those devils. And your given name reminds me of that fact every time I hear it. I don't give a damn about those bones any more, or even the money that I'm getting paid. I just want to find his remains and give him a Christian burial.' Then, patting the Winchester's stock, he added, 'And I'll kill anything that tries to stop me!'

Joe listened to that with mixed feelings. 'Yeah, well, I can understand that, but don't let your hate get you killed ... or the rest of us. And don't go deliberately looking for trouble. My job is to keep everyone alive, not start a war. There's also the fact that there might not be anything left of Leidy to find. Some hostiles can be a mite hard on an enemy's corpse.' He paused for a long moment to let all that sink in, before asking, 'When did you first realize you two weren't alone up there?'

Mudge blinked rapidly. 'There was some sort of weird horn note that I'd never heard before. Just the once, as though it was a signal ... or maybe a warning. We both thought ... hoped really, that it was a trick of the wind or maybe a wild animal, but deep down we knew it wasn't.' As he finished, he peered curiously at his companion. The eighth-breed scout had raised his eyebrows, as though in recognition of something. 'What is it?' Mudge asked. 'What have I said?'

Joe shrugged. 'Maybe something. Maybe nothing. Only I once heard of a tribe of cave dwellers that used bone horns to communicate with each other. They were called Anasazi. But it couldn't be them. They died out years ago.'

It was late the following afternoon that Cartwright, at the back of the column and now with the advantage of height, first spotted the dust well to their rear. He lost no time in telling his boss.

'I reckon they're about a half day's ride behind us, Mister Marsh.'

'Well at least we now definitely know their intentions,' that man responded. 'They mean to take what's ours!' He was riding at the head of the column, keen to press on and, despite his excess weight, still relatively fresh. And even though they were now up into the foothills, Joe was content to leave the eager scientist there for the present, and allow him the illusion of being in charge for a little bit longer. Since leaving Denver, they had made good time and hadn't encountered any distractions. Such a large party was in little danger from casual banditry, and as yet he hadn't encountered any Indian sign on the old prospecting trail that they were following.

Perversely, it was because Marsh wasn't yet tired that he and Joe had their first run-in. The scout had spotted a perfect, sheltered site to make camp and, even though there was plenty of daylight left, he decided to call a halt for the day. His employer was astonished.

'Don't be ridiculous,' he barked, as he reined in next to Joe. 'We've got ages before the sun goes down, and I want to keep well ahead of Cope!'

Joe regarded the other man steadily. He had known that there would be conflict at some stage. There always was in such a situation, and this seemed as good a time as any to deal with it. After drawing in a deep breath, he stated his case. And, conscious that others were watching, he kept his voice low.

'If this is going to work, Mister Marsh, you *have* to let me do my job. I don't know anything about bones, but I do know how to get us there and back alive. This is only our second day on the trail and we broke camp mighty early, because you had the hots to cover some ground. Well, that's okay, but it makes sense to make camp in daylight, so that we can check over all the animals. Make sure the supplies are evenly distributed and that none of them have any loose shoes or any problems that you didn't spot when you *overpaid* for them!'

Marsh began to splutter, so his scout moved on swiftly. 'As for those *hombres* following us. Well they're always going to be out there, but they won't try anything anytime soon. If all they want is the bones, they'll wait until we've done all the hard work and then make a play for them on the way back. Makes sense, huh? So what all this means, is that I'm doing the job you paid me for. And if this isn't going to work out between us, I'll draw my pay and turn back now. It's your choice!'

How long his employment would now last was any

man's guess, because the scientist was staring at him in wide-eyed disbelief. That man's brow furrowed deeply, pressing the skin back on his bald head. His mouth opened and closed a couple of times, as he absorbed everything that had been said. The fact that he had actually paid attention though, was proven by his next remark.

'So you really don't believe that Cope's bruisers are any threat to us at present?'

Joe shook his head patiently. 'As I've just said, for my money, they'll let us recover the bones and move in on the way back to Denver. If they're not bothered about some blood-letting and it works out for them, they'll even get some mules for free. We'll just have to make sure that doesn't happen, won't we? So it's what's waiting over yonder in those mountains that you need to worry about. But I've got a surprise up my sleeve if those hostiles try anything.'

Othniel Marsh gazed long and hard at his resolute employee, before momentarily glancing at Cartwright. Whatever he saw obviously convinced him because, finally, he emphatically nodded.

'You'll stay hired until I say otherwise, and I *will* follow your advice . . . just don't mention those damn mules again!'

The two men sat on the hillside, well away from any of the campfires, so as to retain their night vision. Far off across the darkened landscape, they could make out specks of light, but unlike the stars twinkling above, these were man made.

'I'd like to go down there and pick a few of them bastards off,' muttered Cartwright. 'Send them slinking back to Denver with a bloody nose.'

Joe nodded sympathetically. 'Only problem is, Colorado's a state now. It's got law and order and all the shit that goes with it. I don't think Marsh would appreciate a murder warrant following him back east.'

His companion chuckled quietly. 'I'd certainly give him something new to worry about, but happen you're right. That's why Marsh didn't fire you this afternoon. He can be stubborn and impatient, but he's basically a fair man. He saw the sense in what you had to say.'

'You've obviously worked for him before.'

'Yeah. He's done other bone-hunting trips, but nothing like this one.'

'And what about that mute assistant of his,' Joe queried. 'I ain't heard that Hayden fella say one damn thing all day long.'

Cartwright grunted. 'Marsh took to him at the university, but I've got to say that . . .'

The single, powerful gunshot crashed out with stunning clarity, and both men reacted with practised speed. As startled cries echoed around the hillside, they each closed one eye and took off in opposite directions around the edge of the camp. From further up the trail, there came a second detonation and a momentary muzzle flash.

'Don't nobody else fire,' Joe bellowed out, as he scrambled towards the source. 'And stay low!'

In the flickering glow of a campfire, he could just make out a shock of white hair. Mudge! The man was apparently aiming at something, because again the Winchester discharged. Finally Joe reached him, and grabbing hold of the warm barrel, he shoved the carbine skyward. 'Stop shooting, God damn it!'

Ben Mudge turned to face him, his eyes wild. 'Didn't you see them? They're out there in the dark.'

Only then did the scout open his other eye and search the surrounding hillside. Even with perfect night vision, he couldn't see a single living thing. Cartwright joined them, and barked out, 'Could it have been a wolf, or maybe a Bighorn sheep? The night can play tricks on you.'

Mudge frantically shook his head. 'No, no, it's them. They've come for us!'

Joe regarded him sceptically. 'Dave, take him over to a fire.' Then, as Marsh uncertainly approached them, he called out, 'I'll go take a look-see. I'll call out before I show myself again. Just make sure nobody else gets trigger happy, yeah?' With that, the scout moved sure-footedly off into the gloom, his new Winchester at the ready. The sawn-off that he habitually carried remained slung across his back. Such a weapon was best suited to short-range work, when he knew exactly what he was up against.

He advanced carefully for about a hundred yards or so, before halting and dropping into a crouch, his carbine resting easily in the crook of his left arm. The others were far enough away for him to exclude them from his thoughts. Breathing softly, he remained motionless and willed himself to blend into the landscape. Even though the moon was at the beginning of its cycle, and therefore merely a slim crescent, there was just enough natural light for him to scrutinize his surroundings.

He knew that with the campfires casting their flickering light on the various rock formations, Ben Mudge could easily have allowed his fevered imagination to take over. After all, he and his doomed companion had been attacked in darkness and next to a fire.

Time passed without incident, and the lure of a mug of coffee grew stronger. Joe had just about determined that Mudge's inner demons had obviously got the better of him, because there was quite simply nothing visible on the damned hillside – and then, as he was on the point of returning to the camp, his peripheral vision caught a slight hint of movement further up the trail. Most men would have missed it for sure, but Joe had spent his adult life out in the wilds. Although he didn't yet know whether it was man or beast, the sudden realization that they were definitely not alone brought a tingling chill to his flesh.

Taking a snap decision, he swiftly rose to his feet and launched himself forwards. Up ahead, a shadowy *upright* figure reacted instantly, and raced off in the direction of Platte Canyon. Even though hampered by the rough terrain and trying to avoid breaking his ankles amongst the stones, Joe kept up a rapid pace – but he might as well have been standing still, because

41

whoever he was chasing was as swift and nimble as a wolf. Cursing, he juddered to a halt, and tucked the Winchester's butt into his shoulder. For the briefest of moments he drew a bead on his fleeing two-legged prey. His finger tightened on the trigger – but then, with a frustrated grunt, he abruptly lowered the weapon. He was breathing far too heavily to fire accurately, and there was little point in alarming his companions for no gain. And he had achieved something, because whoever was out there, now knew that he had to keep his distance, even at night.

Reluctantly turning away, Joe slowly padded back downhill until he came within range of the firelight. 'Hello the camp,' he called out, spreading his arms away from his sides as though in supplication. 'I'm coming in.'

The second that the returning scout was visible, Marsh called out, 'Well, did you see anything?' And then, gesturing at his white-haired collector, he added, 'Or is this man dreaming?'

Joe waited until he was close enough to gently place a hand on Mudge's right shoulder. 'Oh, there was someone out there all right. Ben might have over-reacted a bit, but he's definitely not going mad! And what that means is that from now on until we return to Denver, everyone will have to take turns at guard duty. There's plenty of us, so it won't be too tough.'

Edward Drinker Cope unhappily paced back and forth in front of the fire, pausing occasionally to glance up into the foothills. For all his apparent ferocity, he was also a deeply insecure man. And one thing that really got under his skin was 'not knowing' – not knowing exactly where the new fossil find was, and not knowing what had just happened up there in the dark.

'I might only be a mere palaeontologist,' he barked out sarcastically, 'but I know the sound of gunfire when I hear it. Something's amiss up there!'

Six other men sat around the campfire warily observing him, but it was the one with a misshapen nose and heavy bruising around his eyes who answered: 'Who cares, boss? They're probably just shooting at shadows. And if they have met trouble, well, that's their problem . . . *ain't it?*'

Grinding to a halt, Cope stared at him silently for a time, as he composed a suitable response. He loathed the necessity for his involvement with such characters. To someone of his background, the so-called 'hired guns' were really just the gutter sweepings of the frontier. But unfortunately, if he was to make his name as the greatest fossil hunter of his age, he had temporary need of them. By locating such a treasure trove, that charlatan Marsh had managed to obtain a big advantage. If he were to return east with a massive haul of dinosaur bones, then the game would be up. Cope sighed bitterly. Life just wasn't fair. And that fact meant that he couldn't play fair. Hence his eventual reply.

'You've already encountered that damned half-breed. He doesn't seem like the sort of man who would shoot at shadows.' He pointedly waited for a moment until the other man, going by the name of Perry Jakes, had grudgingly acknowledged that fact. 'So I need to know if they are in trouble up there. Remember, I know those bones are in the Rockies, but not exactly where. If anything happens to Marsh and his people, all this is for nothing and none of you will collect your bonus.'

Jakes showed exactly what he thought of that prospect by spitting a dark stream of tobacco on to the hard ground. 'So what do you want me to do . . . boss?'

Cope hadn't missed that slight insolent hesitation. 'Get up close and keep an eye on them,' he retorted. 'Become a solid shadow, but try not to get shot at. If you see anything that doesn't look right, drop back and wait for the rest of us.'

The gun thug relished that even less. 'The only way for me to get near, is to ride right through the night. If I try it in daylight, they'll pick me up for sure.' Cope's lavish facial hair expanded, as he favoured him with a smile that contained little good will. 'Well then, you'd better get going, hadn't you?'

The new day found Marsh's column continuing its gruelling journey up to Platte Canyon. The rocky terrain provided little in the way of shade, and with the sun burning down relentlessly they soon felt as though they had entered a furnace. Not one of the ten men realized that shortly before daybreak they had acquired a discreet tail. After the night's events, all eyes were on the landscape ahead; even those of Joe Eagle and 'Buckskin' Dave, who should definitely have known better, although in fairness the spy kept well back.

'Do you believe that even now we are in danger?' Marsh queried, his anxiety plain to see. He had moved ahead of the others to join Joe, who was riding point. That man glanced at him before continuing to scan his surroundings.

'Whoever it was last night knows that we are alert, so I reckon he or maybe *they* will keep their distance. What worries me is Platte Canyon. The narrowest stretch is about eight miles long, with walls up to a thousand feet high. It's the perfect place for them to get the drop on us.' The scout gave a slight chuckle, but the mild humour had been totally lost on his employer.

'Can't we go around it?' Marsh almost pleaded.

Joe shook his head. 'Not if you want to collect those bones sometime this year. All we can do is go through at widely spaced intervals, leading two mules apiece. That way, if they try a rock fall, at least the whole group won't get wiped out.'

Marsh was aghast. 'That's not very encouraging, Mister Eagle.'

Joe was unrepentant. 'It wasn't meant to be. I'm trying to get you to realize that this isn't some sort of picnic you've set out on. There's hostiles ahead of you who will definitely kill you to stop you taking their bones, and there's other folks behind you who'll quite likely do the same to take them from you. It'll be kill, or be killed, because that's just the way it is sometimes. Oh, and the name's Joe. *Mister* Eagle has me looking for the warrant in your hand!'

The other man offered a weak smile. 'So, Joe, you're sure that those Indians are protecting the bones and aren't just dangerous because we're invading their land?'

The scout emphatically shook his head. 'From what Ben has said, they've arranged them in a huge pattern, as though in some sort of heathen ceremony. I reckon they see them as sacred and worth killing to protect. *And* they know that he escaped, which is why they came this far out of the mountains to keep watch.'

The scientist expelled a great gust of air, rather like a horse. 'I'm beginning to realize that Mister Cartwright was spot on about you. I just hope that we all live to tell the tale!'

CHAPTER FOUR

It took the whole of that third day to reach the beginning of Platte Canyon. On either side of it, cliffs reared up out of the foothills that were hopelessly unscalable with animals. It was only then that Marsh truly understood why traversing the great chasm was their only option. He offered not a word of protest when Joe Eagle gave the command to make camp outside the canyon, next to the fast-flowing South Platte river. Joe did, however, explain his reasoning.

'We're safest out in the open, with some space around us. And enjoy it while you can, because from now on we're going to be surrounded by the high stuff.'

As the teamsters tended to the animals and the others constructed a cooking fire, Joe wandered over to the river to fill his canteen. The water, straight off the mountains, was cold and beautifully clean. He reflected there was a lot to be said for living up in the high country, so long as one could tolerate the seemingly endless and truly punishing winters.

His eyes drifted over to the mouth of the canyon. God help them if it all went wrong in there, yet short of travelling the rest of the way on foot without any animals there really was no alternative. But that was for the following day. First of all they had to get through the night!

Perry Jakes was beginning to rue the day he had ever met Edward Drinker Cope. First of all he had had his nose broken by some God-damned half-breed, and now he had to endure a solitary cold camp in the foothills of the Rockies. And such was the height above sea level that once the sun went down it was *really* cold. It would be hard to sleep without lighting a fire, and due to riding through much of the previous night he hadn't managed any at all then.

To his jaundiced mind, the solitary mission was a complete waste of time. There had been no more shooting and no sign of any threat to the rival column. Not that he'd been able to get very close during the day, for fear of being spotted. And now, as he sat shivering in a single blanket, he had only beef jerky and some admittedly delicious pemmican to sustain him.

As he sourly stared up the hillside at the distant but very inviting campfire, he tried hard to dismiss thoughts of a mug of piping hot coffee. Just as on so many occasions before, he felt hard done by. His ma, a gentle soul, had named him Perry after the famous naval hero, Commodore Matthew Calbraith Perry, hoping that such a start would send her son on to certain success. Unfortunately, she died when he was six, and he never really took to his pa, who was a violent, abusive man, prone to beating his only son with a knotted plough line. Like so many others, Perry had run away and joined the Union army for the generous bounty on offer, and afterwards had ended up as a dissolute 'gun for hire', drifting wherever the work took him. And right now it had taken him to a desolate hillside, miles from anywhere, with no one to talk to and no hot vittles.

Stuffing some more pemmican into his mouth, Jakes peered miserably around. His horse was both hobbled and ground tethered to a rock, because the last thing he needed was to end up on foot. The animal glanced at him, as though somehow sharing his gloomy mood. Then, quite suddenly, its ears pricked up and it began to whinny nervously.

'What is it, boy?' murmured Jakes, his dissatisfaction abruptly forgotten. 'What have you heard?' Even as he spoke, he twisted around searching for anything that could have disturbed the animal.

Without any firelight to affect his sight, the gun thug had perfect night vision, but by the time he picked out the rapid movement it was already too late. As a strange figure rose up from the rocks and surged towards him, Jakes desperately reached for his holstered Remington. Although sitting down, he cleared leather with customary speed. Yet before he even had a chance to cock the single-action weapon, the apparition was upon him. Some form of curved edge hacked viciously at his throat, and quite suddenly it was all over for Perry Jakes.

With his chest suddenly drenched in sticky liquid, he toppled sideways, his gun falling from nerveless fingers. Barely slowing down, the shadowy form moved on to the tethered horse. Dimly, Jakes watched his killer slash at the neck of the helpless animal and the dying man tried to cry out, but no sound would come, only more blood. And then his eyes closed forever.

Fed and watered and having passed a relatively uneventful night, Marsh's column was preparing to enter Platte Canyon. And yet there was little peace of mind amongst the group. All had heard the strange, anguished cry of some animal off in the darkness on their back trail. Unsurprisingly, even with the advent of daylight, no one had felt inclined to investigate, because it was the ordeal ahead of them that consumed their thoughts.

Each man, including their esteemed leader, had his own horse and two mules to get through the canyon. They were to go through at widely spaced intervals, with Joe being the first to attempt it, and all the others in the required order to follow on. 'Buckskin' Dave Cartwright would be last, and he was already feeling lonely.

'You just watch,' he complained only half jokingly. 'Those tarnal Indians will wait until there's just me left and then try something.'

Joe, his eyes on an increasingly agitated Ben Mudge, lowered his voice so that only Cartwright would hear. 'For my money, if anything's going to happen, it'll be when there's half of us through. If they can somehow split the column in two, we'll be in big trouble.'

His next remarks were diplomatically addressed to Othniel Marsh, but they were loud enough for everyone to hear. 'Unless you're on the move, I want everyone's eyes up there, on the rims. You see anyone moving, you open up with those Winchesters, pronto!'

It was then that Tom Hayden, obviously spooked and out of his element, spoke up for the first time that day . . . or even possibly since Denver.

'Seems to me that we should all go through at once, at speed and take them by surprise. That's if there's even anyone up there, which I very much doubt.'

Marsh peered at his assistant in astonishment, uncertainty suddenly clouding his bearded features. Glancing at Joe he hesitantly remarked, 'Perhaps there is something in what he says, Mister Eagle . . . *Joe*. After all, what if some of us get separated?'

The scout sighed. He didn't have time for unnecessary distractions and so his response was harsher than he intended. 'Your problem, Mister Hayden, is that you ain't got a clue what you're up against. Part of that canyon floor is just a narrow path next to the river. We go barrelling in there like a mob and we'll end up with more broke legs than you've had hot vittles. Now get in line, mind your mules, and move when you're told to!' He glanced sharply at Marsh, who reluctantly nodded his assent. It was time.

Joe's right hand held the reins to his horse, whilst his left held two lengths of rope with which to lead the mules. It meant that he was fully occupied, but he couldn't risk tethering the animals in a row in case one of them ended up in the river and dragged the others along. Therefore, as he moved into the canyon proper, he felt an uncomfortable vulnerability. His sawn-off was looped over the saddle horn, so in an emergency he would just have to leave the animals to their own devices.

His progress was unnerving. The deeper in that he advanced, the more the walls closed in on him, and because the canyon possessed a number of gentle curves he could soon no longer see the others. The rough track drew nearer and nearer to the fast-flowing river and he had no option but to follow it. The combined noise from the watercourse and the three animals' hoofs in such a constricted space, meant that he likely wouldn't even hear anything happening above him.

After he'd travelled a few hundred yards, he turned in the saddle and bellowed, 'Next!' He could only trust that the others would follow on and do likewise, which was why he had instructed Cartwright to take last place. He, too, was a man of the west, and would understand what was required.

The narrowest, most dangerous stretch was less than a mile long, but it seemed to take an age to pass through. His neck ached from constantly swivelling around, searching for trouble. And then, amazingly, the canyon began to open out again and he was past the worst. It was at that point that he came to a sudden decision. Rather than continue as he had planned, he would wait around for some of the others to join him, because some sixth sense told him that any attack would come on the stretch that he had just covered.

Ground tethering the animals with a heavy rock, he slung the shotgun over his shoulder and cocked the Winchester. Waiting impatiently, he watched as the next rider came into view. It was one of the teamsters who, although competent in his handling of the animals, was displaying signs of anxiety. His relief on sighting Joe was plain to see.

'It'll be Marsh next, yeah?' the scout called out.

'No. That Hayden fella was getting kind of skittish with the waiting around, so he's following me.'

Joe shrugged. He guessed it really didn't matter, so long as they all made it. But then came the rapid clatter of hoofs and he cursed. 'That silly bastard's riding way too fast. He'll lose control for sure!' And that was exactly what happened.

As Marsh's assistant came around the last bend it was obvious that he was travelling far too rapidly for the conditions. Suddenly catching sight of the two men waiting for him, he panicked and reined in hard. One of the following mules collided with his mount's hindquarters. The horse fell sideways taking Hayden with it, whilst the mule veered uncontrollably off to the right and plunged straight into the South Platte.

Thoroughly spooked, the other mule kept on

running, hurtling past Joe and the teamster and on through the canyon. Hayden lay still on the ground, apparently stunned by the heavy fall. Seething with anger, Joe drew his Bowie knife and raced over to the suffering creature. A gunshot would have been easier and less messy, but he didn't want to advertise their position. Steeling himself against the unnecessary killing, he sawed at the animal's neck.

As a geyser of blood burst forth, he shifted to one side and regretfully wiped his blade clean on the twitching body. Then Hayden groaned and began to come round. Joe angrily turned on him, but before he could say anything, the teamster called out, 'Marsh is on his way through. I'll go and warn him before . . . sweet Jesus!'

From up on the rim there came a tremendous rumbling sound, as though the Earth itself was on the move. And to some extent it was: a great jumble of rocks, large and small, cascaded down at the canyon's narrowest point. Three figures were briefly visible, but they were the least of Joe's concerns.

'Ride like the devil!' he bellowed at the startled scientist, who had just come into view.

As gunshots rang out from those still waiting their turn, Marsh suddenly realized the danger and, releasing the mules, frantically dug in his heels. He only just made it. With a tremendous crash, the falling rocks hit the trail just behind him, sending up a cloud of dust and effectively blocking it. The terrifying noise from so close to them panicked the pack animals. Yanking the lines from his grasp, they raced off at full pelt, but this time the teamster was ready. Leaping at the nearest, he seized it around its neck and wrestled the frightened beast to a halt.

Marsh managed to rein in his horse and turned to view the result of the rock fall. The track was effectively blocked and he was now separated from the rest of his men. Hot lead had cleared the rim, but that didn't mean that the figures weren't still up there, ready to hurl more missiles down on the white men. All in all, it was quite a mess!

As the teamster tethered his mule to another large rock, Joe instructed, 'Get your Winchester and cover this end of the canyon. You too, Mister Marsh. Now they've split us up, they might just try to rush us.'

That man tore his eyes from the rock fall. 'You think this has all been pre-planned?'

Joe didn't hold back. 'God damn right I do. From the moment one of them stalked our campfire I reckoned they were out to stop us getting anywhere near their precious bones. All this just proves it. They know these mountains like the back of their hands, so they'll know when to strike and when to move.' Abruptly he ceased talking and turned away towards the river.

Marsh couldn't hide his anxiety. 'Where are you going?'

'To think.'

For long moments he stared in silence at the fast-flowing water, before coming to a decision. Then, as voices sounded off beyond the blockade, he moved into action. Not even bothering to look at Hayden as that man staggered to his feet, Joe trotted over to the rocks and began to climb them. It was comparatively easy for him to get to the top, but he recognized that they would have no chance of getting the animals over. And then a stone the size of a baby's head crashed into rock mere inches away and he knew that whatever they were going to do it would have to be fast.

Peering over the man-made summit, he found himself face to face with Dave Cartwright. 'This sure is a hell of a thing, ain't it?' that man drolly remarked, before yelling at those behind him. 'Work those Winchesters, God damn it. Even if you can't see anybody, just shoot.'

'Dave, I need you to do something for me.'

'Yo!'

'Get your people and animals well back, away from these rocks. There's going to be one heck of an explosion.'

'Say what?'

'An explosion, damn it,' Joe exclaimed impatiently. 'Just do as I say, otherwise we might as well ride double back to Denver right now and forget the whole thing!'

Cartwright's eyes widened expressively, but he had the sense not to prevaricate. Turning away, he retreated down the rock pile, all the while shouting instructions. 'You teamsters get all the animals back down the trail a-ways. Ben. You and me will follow on, but we've got to keep laying some fire down on that rim. Savvy?'

Joe didn't hear the response to that, because he, too, was clambering back down to the trail. The teamster had followed instructions and was standing guard, whereas Marsh was fussing over his assistant. 'His left forearm's broken, Joe. We need to tend to him.'

The scout completely ignored them, instead racing over to one of his tethered mules. Even as he did so, another rock smashed down nearby. Unfastening one of the packs, he withdrew a sizeable bundle of cylindrical red tubes, bound together by strips of rawhide.

'Sweet Jesus,' muttered the teamster. 'Have we been hauling that stuff around since Denver?'

'You're gonna thank me for it in a minute,' Joe retorted. Displaying it clearly to his employer, he instructed, 'You and Hayden had better be well clear of here before this blows or you'll have more than a broken arm to worry about.' With that, he returned to the barrier and began to pull rocks aside at the bottom of it, so that he could get the parcel of dynamite well into it. All the time he worked, shots rang out as Cartwright and Mudge carried out a fighting withdrawal. They were unlikely to hit anything, but at least it kept their assailants' heads down.

With sweat pouring off his face, Joe finally got the explosives wedged deep inside the rock fall. After glancing around to make sure that the others were clear, he pulled a small waterproof package from a pocket and extracted one of his precious Lucifers. As the 'fire stick' flared into life, he held it against the end of a fuse and was immediately rewarded with a vivid response. All he had to do then was run for his life.

Another missile crashed down nearby, but that was suddenly the least of Joe's problems. With his heart pumping like the bellows in a blacksmith's forge, he charged along the track to rejoin his three companions.

As the breathless demolitionist dropped down next to them, the only detonation came from an occasional gunshot. He could only pray that the fuse hadn't gone out, because he sure as hell wasn't going back to check on it.

Marsh favoured him with a quizzical glance. 'How did you know what length of fuse to use?'

Joe shrugged. 'I didn't. It's the first time I ever set a match to that stuff. Kind of makes you think, don't it?'

Before his stunned employer could respond, an ear-splitting roar rent the air and the ground seemed to tremble beneath them.

CHAPTER FIVE

'What in God's name is that?'

Edward Drinker Cope and his five men had spent the morning moving up through the foothills towards the entrance to Platte Canyon. For some time their cautious progress had been accompanied by the sound of muted gunfire. Then they beheld the unexpected sight of a mule struggling helplessly against the strong current of the South Platte River, as it was swept out of the canyon and back down towards Denver. But none of that disturbed them anything like as much as their latest discovery.

Close by the blood-soaked body of Perry Jakes's horse lay the disgusting, fly-covered pile of offal that had prompted Cope's question. Then the answer graphically presented itself when they came across the butchered carcass of Jakes himself. Or at least they presumed it was he, because it was mostly just a pile of flesh, sinew and hair. All the major bones had been removed and taken . . . somewhere!

One of the men immediately voided his stomach,

whilst even their leader, who was used to dissecting dead creatures, turned a pasty grey. The dead man's buddy, Brad Dix, stared at the remains in horror. He had been harbouring doubts about their current employment ever since he and Jakes had been easily bested by the half-breed in town, and this only confirmed them.

'Who'd do something like this to him?' he asked in hushed tones. 'It just ain't human.'

His boss was deep in thought. The scientist hadn't really counted on someone in his employ actually *dying*, and the reality of it had badly shaken him. Even so, Cope hadn't yet lost the capability for logical deliberation. He had noted with great surprise that the various incisions had been made by some sort of primitive cutting tool, rather than a sharp knife. And, although unsure of the significance, he also noticed that Jakes' weapons had merely been discarded near the human detritus. Such items were obviously low on his killers' list of priorities. 'Presumably it's the same individuals that are in conflict with Marsh in the canyon,' he remarked. 'It appears that Ben Mudge's story about murderous savages protecting the bones wasn't just an invention to increase his pay.'

His employees peered at him apprehensively. It was the first they'd heard about any savages, murderous or otherwise. 'We didn't sign on as no Indian fighters, Mister Cope,' Dix protested. 'You said we were just stealing some old bones from a rival.'

Realizing that he had said too much, Cope sighed

regretfully. This was undoubtedly going to cost him dear. Gazing around at his frontier flotsam, he was just on the point of responding when a tremendous muffled roar emanated from the depths of the canyon. The detonation was powerful enough to cause surrounding rocks to vibrate.

Dix glanced nervously at his companions and gulped. He had a sinking feeling in his gut that told him things were only going to get worse!

The rock pile, so recently dumped on to the trail, erupted back into the air like a volcano, but a great cloud of dust masked most of the stunning sight. As displaced matter again fell to earth, the deafening noise seemed to go on forever. Smaller fragments smacked down some distance from the explosion, but Joe and his companions were well clear of it all. As for the others, he could only hope that 'Buckskin' Dave had taken his warning seriously.

They all watched anxiously as the dust finally began to settle on a changed landscape. It was immediately apparent that the river was partially dammed, but that counted for little. What really mattered was the trail, and so they all heaved a collective sigh of relief when finally they were able to observe the result of Joe's great gamble. A path had been blasted through the rubble that would allow free access in either direction, which meant that their probable future escape route was safeguarded as well. And, after such a display of awesome power, it was unlikely that their assailants would attempt to block the canyon again.

'Very well done, Joe,' Marsh announced. 'It appears that we're back in business.'

'There's something else, as well,' that man responded as he stared up at the rim. 'We're not under attack anymore. Seems like those fellas haven't come up against dynamite before. Which means we need to get the hell out of here while the going's good!'

'What about my arm?' Hayden wailed.

Joe glanced at him scathingly. 'You broke it, you fix it!'

But of course it didn't work out that way. As the rest of the party came into view, Marsh responded, 'This man works for me and is my responsibility. We must set his arm before we move on.'

Joe sighed with annoyance, but said to the team-ster, 'There's some strips of timber on the pack animals. Grab a couple of them and some rope. They'll answer as a splint.' With that, he strode off to attend to more important matters.

Through the settling dust, Cartwright appeared at the head of the others, sporting a hugely infectious grin. 'Sweet Jesus, you don't mess about do you? I'll warrant those bastards shit themselves when that stuff went off. You got some more, by any chance?'

The scout couldn't help but chuckle. 'I've got a few tubes left, just in case things turn really nasty.'

The other man nodded, his expression suddenly deadly serious. 'That seems likely. How many mules did we lose?'

'Three – one down the river and two into the hills. And Hayden's horse. Broke a leg, because he panicked. There was payback, though – they're splinting his arm now.'

With perfect timing, Marsh's assistant howled with pain. The two men favoured each other with knowing glances.

'If this trip gets rougher, that arm'll likely infect and we'll end up sawing it off,' Cartwright remarked in a deadpan fashion, his voice low so as not to reach Ben Mudge. That individual had handled both the mules and his carbine proficiently, but his features were noticeably strained, as though too many bad memories were coming back to haunt him. If he had known what awaited them, he might well have followed the lone mule on its watery journey back to Denver!

It was late in the day by the time the weary expedition finally emerged from Platte Canyon. Even though there had been no further incidents, they uttered a collective sigh of relief at getting clear of its forbidding, high-sided walls. Not that the terrain would get any easier. Quite the opposite in fact, because they were now faced by the snow-capped mountains that formed the Rampart Range, and the only way was up . . . and up.

After carefully scrutinizing the two scientists, Joe decided to order a halt for the day. Hayden, now mounted on a mule, was white-faced and swaying in his saddle. The shock of breaking an arm had obviously taken its toll, and it was also probably true that he had never been under deadly threat before. As for Marsh, well some of his earlier bluster had subsided, as the harsh reality of their task had finally sunk in. The wilds of the Colorado Rockies were indeed a far cry from New Haven, Connecticut!

They made camp in a small clearing, with the river on their right. All around them lay great boulders that appeared to have been there since time began. Since the Anasazi, if that was who they were, undoubtedly already knew the location of the white men, there was little point in tolerating a cold camp. Hayden especially needed warmth and hot food, but Joe tempered that with hard logic.

'Keep the cooking fires small and stay low. And no unnecessary movement. No sense in making yourselves a target.' With that, he hefted his weapons and moved off on foot, followed by Cartwright. As on the previous night, both men left the chores to the teamsters and prowled around the perimeter for a while, getting their bearings before darkness fell.

'What made you pick a Schofield?' Cartwright suddenly enquired, proving that he really didn't miss much.

Without taking his eyes off their surroundings, Joe nevertheless smiled and patted the holstered revolver. 'With the top break, it reloads faster than anything else out there. Sometimes that can count for a lot . . . and it puts down what it hits.'

His companion nodded thoughtfully. 'After what happened today, you might have to prove that!'

Night had fallen and the hot meal was long gone. Hours of darkness stretched ahead of them. The two fires provided necessary warmth, but flickering shadows played tricks on frayed nerves. And Hayden's moaning was really beginning to rankle. Marsh had dosed him with some laudanum, but his arm was badly broken and the pain simply wouldn't let up.

'For Christ's sake,' one of the teamsters exclaimed. 'You keep bitching like this an' we'll have to gag you!'

'Ain't no one getting gagged on my watch,' Cartwright angrily retorted.

Something else was bothering Joe Eagle. The animals, tethered close by, were displaying a restlessness that had nothing to do with Tom Hayden's pathetic bleating. Working on the basis that anything out there was an enemy, the scout surreptitiously muffled his shotgun's action with a blanket and retracted both hammers.

Slightly chastened, the irritable teamster clambered to his feet to stoke the fire.

'Get down, God damn it,' Joe hissed, but he was too late: a stone-headed axe flew out of the gloom and buried itself deep in the standing man's back. With an agonized howl, he flung up his arms in a reflex action and pitched forwards into the flames. As the sickly sweet smell of burning flesh wafted around the camp, Joe rolled to his left and levelled the deadly sawn-off. He had a rough idea of where the hatchet had originated and so reacted accordingly.

With the butt tucked tightly into his shoulder, he squeezed one trigger. The big gun discharged with an awesome crash and then he swung it slightly to one side and fired the second barrel. This time he was rewarded with a scream that was music to his ears. Rapidly turning over on to his back, Joe broke open the shotgun and replaced the empty cartridges. Then he rolled a couple more times and leapt to his feet.

Leaving the others to see to the writhing teamster, he moved off at a right-angle, because only a fool would race blindly into the dark directly after a wounded assailant. As he walked away from the firelight, his eyes slowly adapted to the gloom. He had no idea how many he was up against, but with his 'crowd pleaser' cocked and ready, he felt the equal of anything he might encounter. The camp was almost out of sight when he heard a vague scuffling sound somewhere in the distance and decided it was time to 'cut' trail.

Angling off to his left, with every sense on heightened alert, Joe moved forwards through the rocks, traversing his gun from side to side. Then his peripheral vision suddenly picked up a slight glistening on a stone surface up ahead. With his heart beating rapidly in anticipation, the scout cautiously closed in. He gained grim satisfaction from what he discovered.

Blood. A very great deal of blood in fact, splashed

over rocks and in the dust. For there to be so much, his victim's wound had to be mortal, especially so far from civilization. It was that realization that motivated his next move. Without any hesitation, he backed up towards the camp. There was ample noise to guide his steps, allowing him to continue facing his surroundings. When he was only a short distance away, he wisely stopped and called out, 'Hello the camp,' before continuing.

The others all stared at him expectantly, but his initial concern was solely for the teamster. Consequently, he shook his head in dismay at the sight that awaited him. The man had been dragged out of the fire and was sprawled nearby, covered in blood and quite dead. The ghastly burns to his face only seemed to emphasize the awful fact that the expedition had just suffered its first fatality.

It was Cartwright who finally broke the silence. 'Did you get the bastard?'

Joe nodded. 'Badly wounded and like to die. I left him to it.'

The other man nodded his understanding – but not so their leader. 'That's madness! He's just murdered one of my men and you let him get away! I demand that you to go back out there and finish him off – in fact, I want to see the body!'

Joe's eyes briefly met Cartwright's, before he concentrated all his attention on Marsh. Moving closer, so they were almost nose to nose, he spoke softly, but not a man there missed a single word. 'There sure ain't no sense in that, Mister Marsh. The amount of blood makes it odds on that he's finished. He'll just crawl off and die some place. *But,* if I was to try and follow him in the dark, he'd fight like a cornered animal. So if you want to see a body, you go out and look for it, because I sure as hell ain't!'

As his scout turned away heading for the nearest coffee pot, Marsh was speechless, but that man hadn't quite finished. 'Oh, and from now on all hot food will be eaten in daylight. We'll have to huddle up tight at night, because there'll be no more fires. They make us way too vulnerable.'

No one even commented when Joe made a minor detour to recover the dead teamster's hat and jacket. They all assumed that he intended to use them to keep warm during the nights ahead, but as was usual with him, he was thinking far deeper than that.

The events of the previous night had obviously weighed heavily on Othniel Marsh, because the new day found him with deep shadows under his red, bleary eyes. As soon as the camp was fully awake, he made directly for the individual who had apparently effortlessly assumed leadership of the expedition.

'I have decided to turn back. No amount of dinosaur bones are worth the loss of men's lives!'

Joe was astounded and he made no attempt to hide the fact. 'One man has *already* lost his life. If we turn back now, he will have died for nothing. Think on that!'

Marsh's eyelids flickered rapidly. 'Oh, I have been. It's just that I didn't . . . realize what it would be like.'

'Then it must be different with you folks back east,' Joe scoffed. 'Because out on the frontier, when you commit to something, you damn well finish it. I agreed to do a job for you and I'm gonna do it. So don't go backing out on me now, 'cause I need the money!'

The scientist rocked on his heels slightly, as though taken aback by the vehemence of the other man's opinion. And before he had chance to respond, Ben Mudge suddenly stepped up to the mark.

'There's more than one man dead. Joe Leidy died to bring you knowledge of those dinosaur bones, or had you already forgotten that? And look at my hair! It didn't turn white on account of the mountain air. We told you this was going to be dangerous. That's why you bought all these fancy Winchesters. They ain't toys, you know. So let's use them to kill those cockchafers. I might be scared as hell, but it's why I've come along. I want payback!' He paused for a moment, as another thought occurred to him. 'And do you really want that bastard Cope to find those bones first, because he surely doesn't deserve to!'

With that, he fell silent and turned away, as though exhausted by his outburst. Marsh stared at him for a long moment, before drawing in a deep breath and running a meaty hand over his bearded features. He had clearly not expected such strong resistance from his men. Then he glanced over at the teamster's corpse, as that man's peers constructed a cairn of stones over it to keep the wolves and such away, and his expression hardened.

To Joe's great surprise, his employer abruptly turned to him and uttered just these few words: 'So let's go and find those bones!'

Dizzyingly high up on the mountain side, a lone figure squatted on an isolated outcrop. Heights held no fear for him because he had spent his entire life amongst Colorado's peaks. He possessed sallow, hawk-like features and jet-black hair, worn long down to his shoulders. Beneath his furs lay a lean, muscular frame that included startlingly powerful legs. Years of clambering up and down mountains had endowed him and his kind with almost superhuman endurance and speed.

His attention had been momentarily drawn from the intruders far below to a creature that he held in almost mystical reverence. A golden eagle, boasting a wingspan of some seven feet, glided past his precarious position in search of food. By making use of different currents of air, the magnificent bird of prey could easily travel a hundred miles a day with very little effort. The reverent observer felt a tinge of envy, and it was only with great difficulty that he managed to tear his eyes from the amazing creature and return them to the progress of the hated white men.

In truth, because the Anasazi always kept to the mountain ranges, his kind had mostly managed to avoid contact with them over the years. In the past, occasional trappers and hunters had ventured into the high country, but they had been easily dispatched and their disappearance would doubtless have been attributed to the extreme conditions. It was only now, with the city dwellers' discovery and desire for the ancient relics, that they had come into real contact.

The Indian leader had no doubt that the outcome would be both uncertain and very bloody, because the whites now owned many strange and powerful weapons, including one that could move even rock itself. But there could be no avoiding the conflict, because it was his sworn duty to protect the bones of the gods. Furthermore the trespassers would need to be completely annihilated, otherwise more of their kind, driven by greed, would venture up into the high mountains.

And travelling with them was one man who appeared to possess superior abilities to the rest. He would be dangerous unless stopped, or at least neutralized quickly. To that end, it was time to strike, hard and fast and with overwhelming numbers. And of course that wouldn't be the end of it, because he was well aware that there was a smaller group following on, although he hadn't yet fathomed their purpose.

His mind made up, the Anasazi chief abruptly swivelled sideways and without any hesitation lowered himself over the edge into the yawning void below. After hanging by his fingertips for a moment, he began to swing his body to and fro. Then, with amazing precision and timing, he simply let go. Momentum carried him on to the rock face where his fingers immediately found secure holds, and after

71

that he began the comparatively effortless descent to rejoin his men. It would soon be time to taste the blood of their enemies!

The sun had passed its zenith by the time the six men emerged from the claustrophobic surrounds of Platte Canyon. They soon came upon Marsh's camp-site with its makeshift burial site, and Brad Dix was quick to remove some of the stones at one end.

'Jesus!' he exclaimed, as he took in the charred features. 'Even his own mother wouldn't recognize him. Only the duds tells me it's one of Marsh's men.'

'Yeah. That and the fact that they wouldn't have gone to all that trouble for an Injun,' retorted one of the others scornfully. 'You just fancied a bit of grave robbing, is all.'

Dix flushed scarlet. He was amazed that his motives had been so easily perceived. 'That's a black lie,' he protested. 'You ought to be thanking me. There could have been some heathen lying in wait for us under all this and I'd have smoked him for you.'

'Yeah, yeah,' the other gun thug responded. 'Just put the damn stones back. That could be one of us next, and I'd like to think that somebody would protect my body from the buzzards.'

Dix regarded him resentfully and made no move to comply, because in truth he still hankered after frisking the pockets. It was Cope who finally settled the matter.

'We're Christians one and all . . . or at least I am,

and the dead should be treated respectfully. Cover him up, Dix. Just do it.'

As his employee reluctantly complied, another man by the name of Jared Tiegs spoke up. He'd been prowling around beyond the camp and had made a discovery.

'There's a powerful amount of dried blood over yonder, boss, which would tie in with that sawn-off we heard last night.'

Cope nodded thoughtfully. 'Those savages are getting bolder, and they must know that we're following Marsh and his men. So from now on we'll have to sleep without a fire.' He then added unnecessarily, 'And all of you be on your guard.'

As his men mounted up to move off, Cope uncharacteristically held back until they were all in front of him. From now on, like all wise generals, he intended to lead from the rear!

CHAPTER SIX

Nobody had expected to see the two runaway mules again, certainly not alive, but suddenly they came upon one, apparently tethered to some brushwood beneath an overhanging crag. The braying creature was restrained some distance away from the expedition's steep route, and since they were riding in single file out of necessity, not everyone immediately spotted it. By pure chance it was Marsh who located it first. The loss of three animals had rankled him. He had grown up poor in New York, and hated waste of any kind. So on spying his property, he emitted a grunt of satisfaction and urged his horse out of line towards it.

At that very moment, an unearthly sound echoed around them. Ben Mudge was suddenly wide-eyed with fearful recognition. 'That's what I heard before. . . .'

Joe nodded his understanding. A bone horn! Realizing the danger immediately, he yelled a warning, but his employer was too taken up with recovering his four-legged asset to respond. And so, with remarkable ease, the Anasazi closed their trap. As two warriors leapt into view on the rocky overhang, another half dozen raced around either side of it in two groups of three.

The beefy scientist didn't recognize his deadly peril until it was too late, but his scout was already spurring towards him, closely followed by Ben Mudge. Joe instinctively knew which of his weapons was right for the circumstances. With Marsh directly in front of him, the sawn-off was far too risky and the Winchester too cumbersome at such close range. So, smoothly drawing his Schofield, he took rapid aim at one of the two airborne warriors as they dropped down on to their prey.

The revolver crashed out, abruptly alerting everyone to the fact that they were under attack again. The .45 calibre bullet struck one of the Indians in his chest, immediately taking him out of the fight, but his companion's full weight landed on Marsh and sent the unfortunate man tumbling out of his saddle. The two of them hit the hard ground with sickening force, but it was the white man who bore the full brunt. Winded and almost insensible with shock, he lay completely helpless.

The other warriors closed in around their victim, but strangely made no attempt to strike him. Instead, they seized hold of the stunned scientist and hoisted him aloft. Their intentions were suddenly frighteningly clear.

'They mean to carry him off,' yelled Mudge, but

both white men knew that it was too risky to open fire. It was at that moment that more Anasazi, shrieking like demons, swept in from both ends of the column. This was clearly an all-out assault, and even if they failed to kill every one of the intruders they would still have a valuable hostage.

At the rear of the column, and unaware of Marsh's deadly peril, 'Buckskin' Dave Cartwright knew that at all costs they had to protect the horses. On foot, the whites would be easy prey for their fleet-footed attackers. Slipping out of the saddle, he handed his reins to one of the teamsters and then dropped down behind a boulder. Even though a seasoned frontiersman, he could feel the nerves fluttering in his stomach. It was always like that before a fight.

Strange, dust-coated figures were leaping from rock to rock, shrieking their unintelligible war cries. He couldn't allow them to get in amongst the animals, and so it was time to see just what his new Winchester could really do. Rapidly drawing a bead on the nearest Anasazi, he fired. He could feel the comforting power of the weapon as it discharged, and even better was the sight of his victim crumpling under a mortal blow. Smoothly working the lever action, he fired again and again, all the time shifting to new targets. As sulphurous powder smoke wafted over him, his fear turned to exhilaration. 'Christ, but this is a fine gun,' he muttered gleefully.

Over near the crag, Joe Eagle yelled at his mounted companion Ben Mudge, 'Stay back, until I've broken them up!' He knew that he would be taking a terrible risk, but he simply couldn't allow Marsh to be abducted, because apart from anything else that would render their chances very slim indeed of ever drawing any wages! And from a more charitable viewpoint, it was better by far to kill him in error than condemn him to a possible slow death.

With a savage cry, he spurred his animal forwards, aiming directly at the clutch of warriors carrying his now resisting employer.

Struggling under Marsh's excess weight they did not discern Joe's intention until it was too late. His horse slammed into the closely packed group and sent them spinning like nine-pins. Abruptly unsupported, their captive again crashed to earth, and this time lay completely still.

The seven warriors were momentarily disorientated, and Joe took full advantage of this. His Schofield crashed out time and again, as he emptied the contents of its cylinder at them. Ben Mudge joined in with his carbine, but with two compatriots to avoid, he had to be far more cautious. Then a stone axe, flung from behind, struck the field collector full in his back and sent him plunging forwards off his mount.

With his revolver empty and Mudge likely dead, Joe saw that the situation was indeed desperate. Four warriors had survived his onslaught, although in truth two of them had nasty flesh wounds, but they were all back on their feet and seeking to unhorse him. It was time to take another risk. Holstering his sidearm, he grabbed and cocked the sawn-off. Even as one of them grabbed his ankle, Joe pointed and fired. The full charge struck the doomed Indian in his face at point-blank range, completely destroying his features. As the hands fell away from his ankle, the deadly horseman selected another quarry and squeezed the second trigger.

A concentrated spread of pellets tore into soft flesh, and the sight of another horribly mutilated warrior proved to be too much for the two remaining Anasazi. Oblivious to the fact that the big and terrifying gun was now empty, they broke and fled, leaving their opponent alone in a cloud of powder smoke. He had no time for reflection though, and barely a second to reload, because his companions were still under attack.

Thumbing back the Schofield's top break latch, Joe sharply jerked his hand. As the barrel swung beneath it, the empty cartridge cases literally flew out of the cylinder, allowing him to rapidly refill it. Then, bellowing at one of the teamsters to check on Marsh, he spurred his horse over to Cartwright's position. The scout was completely unaware that the animal handlers were themselves under attack and fighting for their lives, proving that even an experienced fighter could be disorientated in the heat of battle.

'Buckskin' Dave had single-handedly broken the charge on his front. With the barrel of his Winchester literally too hot to touch, the wooden forestock was a Godsend. He had a pile of empty brass cases around him, and was still working the

lever action like a maniac. Broken, bloody bodies littered the ground in front of him, and when Joe
arrived shooting from the saddle, it was enough to
bring the carnage to an end. Perversely, it was at that
very moment that Tom Hayden met with another
accident.

With one arm in a splint, it was all Marsh's assistant
could do to restrain his skittish horse, but he was
determined to join in the fight and assist the teamsters. Ramming the reins between his teeth, he had
finally managed to grab his carbine. Unfortunately,
he had only ever been an indifferent horseman. As
his mount desperately shied away from Cartwright's
fusillade, Hayden entirely lost control and was
thrown from the saddle. With wretched bad luck, his
damaged limb struck a rock, sending him into parox-
ysms of agony that boded ill for the future.

At what had been the front of the column the
frightened teamsters, also armed with Winchesters,
had finally managed to fend off a lighter attack, but
not without sustaining casualties. A blood-soaked
teamster lay dying, with a stone-tipped lance through
his belly, and two more mules had run off.

And then, quite suddenly, it was all over. The surviving Anasazi broke and fled for cover – anywhere to
escape the terrifying 'firesticks' that seemingly never
stopped spitting metal. A number of them lay dreadfully wounded, their groans mingling with those of
Tom Hayden . . . but not for long. As Joe hollered
out, 'Everyone reload, *now*,' Cartwright cautiously
moved amongst the warriors, placing a bullet into

each man's skull. Even though in great pain, those that saw him coming watched implacably, without making any plea for mercy. More than anything else, that told him a great deal about what kind of men they were up against.

Only when his weapons were recharged and he had ensured that the surviving teamsters were in control of the animals, did Joe finally begin to check on the injured. The biggest surprise was Ben Mudge. It transpired that the stone axe had struck him end on, without actually penetrating even his clothing. He had suffered very heavy bruising, but would live to continue avenging Joe Leidy. Othniel Marsh had also survived relatively unscathed. He, too, was badly bruised and had minor cuts on his face and hands, but the main problem seemed to be in his head!

'This is pure lunacy,' he wailed passionately. 'All this killing for a pile of bones!'

'They called it. Happen that'll give 'em pause about trying another full-on attack,' Joe replied, in a chillingly matter-of-fact manner. Although fully aware of Hayden's terrible distress, he had much more that needed saying. 'And think on this. Those fellas don't have any more right to them bones than us, and they certainly ain't gonna stop me drawing my pay! So don't start any more of that turning back shit. Besides, they're behind us now as well, because you can bet your bottom dollar they know about Cope following on. So if we have to fight our way back to Denver anyhow, it might as well be with what we came for.'

Marsh stared at his employee in stunned silence. Although traumatized by the brutal, bloody violence, it hadn't escaped his notice that Joe Eagle had most definitely dropped any pretence at deference. In fact, come to think of it, the last time the scientist had felt fully in control of his own expedition had been back in Denver! With his authority apparently falling away like his mule down the South Platte River, he glanced around and abruptly became aware that Cartwright had joined them. Marsh peered despairingly over at him, hoping to observe some sign – any sign – of support. He was to be sadly disappointed.

Cartwright, blood-spattered and suddenly desperately weary, only had eyes for Joe. He had heard the distinctive reports of the twelve-gauge and knew full well that without him on their flank they would undoubtedly have been overrun.

'That was one hell of a shindig,' he remarked croakily, his mouth unpleasantly dry. 'And one thing's for sure. They weren't Utes. I've had plenty of run-ins with Utes, and they ain't anything like these sons of bitches!'

Joe nodded his agreement. 'Yeah. It don't hardly seem possible, but I reckon they must be Anasazi. What with the stone weapons an' all.'

Cartwright yawned. Reaction had set in, and he was just too tired to be surprised by that revelation. 'Well, whoever they are, I could sleep for a week after that, but I reckon we should move on and find somewhere to make camp for the night. Somewhere more defensible maybe.' Then ominously, he added, 'And that Hayden don't look too good to me. We might just need to work on him some.'

His employer gawped at him uncomprehendingly. 'What on earth do you mean by that?'

Cartwright shrugged, but before he could elaborate, Joe raised another issue. 'We'll need to watch those teamsters as well. They didn't sign on for this kind of work, and losing two buddies has made them kind of edgy. They might decide to cut and run in the dark.'

Now that did register with the increasingly apprehensive scientist. He tried to swallow but his throat, too, had become painfully dry, and he abruptly lost the urge to talk any more. It was shaping up to be quite a night!

'I need to know what's happened up there!' Edward Drinker Cope demanded, not for the first time since leaving Denver. Although the mountains had distorted the sounds of extended heavy gunfire, there was no doubt in his mind that a serious conflict had taken place. And now, even more ominously to his mind, all was silent.

For Brad Dix, the answer was obvious. 'I reckon someone's done to them what the Sioux did to Custer last year.'

Cope was aghast. 'You can't be serious. Marsh has modern weapons and . . . and dynamite.'

The gun hand shrugged. 'That don't always count for much. Up in these mountains, jumped from all sides . . . who knows.'

'Well, I need to. You'll have to steal up there in the dark and find out what took place.'

It was Dix's turn to be horrified. He glanced around at his compatriots for support, but they all seemed to be looking elsewhere. 'Ain't no way I'm going up yonder on my lonesome. No siree! You saw what happened last time. We'd have needed a shovel to collect what was left of Perry!' He paused for an instant. 'Why don't *you* go take a looksee, *Mister* Cope?'

Such insolence could not be tolerated. As he bared his teeth, the scientist's moustache seemed to take on a life of its own. 'When I own a dog, it means I don't have to bark myself, Dix.'

That man's eyes widened. He thought he'd just been insulted, but wasn't quite sure. 'Who you calling a dog?' he asked belligerently.

Cope sighed. All this was achieving nothing. 'I'll pay you one hundred dollars to go up there. How's that sound?'

Dix's eyes expanded even further, until they seemed likely to burst. One hundred dollars American was an awful lot of money for a man of his ilk. Despite his preoccupation, he could also sense his cronies' sudden greedy interest. If he didn't jump in quick, he might easily lose the opportunity. 'In cash?'

His employer was beginning to get exasperated. It was like dealing with a small child. 'Yes, in cash. When we get back to Denver. Because obviously I don't have it on me. There being nothing to spend it on in the mountains.'

Dix nodded slowly. It wasn't the first time in his life that greed had *just* managed to overcome fear.

The coming of darkness signalled the end of another day in the mountains, but not the end of their troubles. It was a fact that nothing seemed to be going well. As Joe had suspected, the teamsters were becoming twitchy, a situation not helped by the discovery that the tethered mule used by the Anasazi to draw in Marsh had been hamstrung, and so was good only for a bullet to the head. And then there was Tom Hayden. The normally taciturn assistant had been making plenty of noise, and all of it related to his broken forearm.

'That last fall finished any chance of the bone knitting together,' Joe murmured to his two companions. 'Hell, it's shattered six ways from Sunday.'

The three men were huddled together in a rocky alcove under a moonlit sky. Theirs was currently a cold camp, but that was about to change.

'What do you suggest?' Marsh queried with obvious trepidation.

Joe was in no doubt about what was required. 'It'll have to come off above the elbow. It's his only chance of survival, 'cause if we leave it be, greenrod will set in and he'll be parolled to Jesus for sure. And I for one wouldn't want a death such as that!'

The expedition leader was clearly horrified as he glanced over to where Ben Mudge was doing his best to comfort the badly injured man. 'There must be *something* else we can do for him,' he almost pleaded.

'Huh,' grunted Cartwright. 'Well, I guess you could start praying, but it didn't ever work for me. Perhaps you've got to be a believer for it to work.'

Joe continued as though neither man had spoken. 'We'll have to risk a fire. With no tar or such, the stump will need cauterizing, and I don't reckon those sons of bitches will come at us again so soon. We took a fearful toll on them today. As for taking the limb, this Bowie of mine will cut through flesh, but it's gonna struggle with bone . . . and we'll need to be quick.'

Surprisingly, it was Marsh who had the answer to that. 'I have a bone saw in my pack.'

Slow on the uptake for once, the others gazed at him in amazement.

'I'm a scientist,' he supplied, 'and we're in these mountains to recover a great many bones. I might wish to cut into some samples – though I certainly never imagined that we'd need to use it on my assistant!'

CHAPTER SEVEN

The three teamsters were supposed to be standing guard, but who could objectively do that at such a time? Their four companions had got a small fire burning and then gently carried Hayden over to it. He was in great distress and seemed completely unaware of what was about to happen. Cartwright kept a small jug of whiskey in his pack for medicinal purposes, and after liberally dosing the patient with it, they poured some over both the knife and the intended point of incision. Next, a leather belt was tied tightly around the patient's upper arm. After exchanging pointed glances, three of the men abruptly placed their full weight on the relevant parts of Hayden's body. Joe drew in a deep breath to steel himself against the expected reaction, and then swiftly made a deep, circular cut through soft flesh.

As Hayden began to scream and scream, the youngest of the trail hands, a man called Tobias, was especially troubled. 'This just ain't right,' he protested to the other two. 'They could have tried splinting that arm again ... or something. What happens if one of *us* gets hurt? Will they cut off *our* arms as well?' With that, he began to edge towards his horse. 'This whole business is going to end badly. If you've got any sense, you'll make a break for it while you can!'

His two buddies stared at him as he untethered the animal, and then quietly led it away from camp. They were torn by indecision. What finally held them in place was a fear of the unknown. Because after all, those heathen maniacs had to be still out there in the darkness somewhere.

Tobias, now unsettlingly alone in that same darkness, had intended walking with his animal for a while. Then Joe got to work with the bone saw and Hayden's tormented shrieks reached a new crescendo, seemingly bouncing off the rock faces. 'The hell with this,' the young man exclaimed, and vaulted into the saddle.

He set off far faster than any rational man should in the mountains at night, and soon had to rein in for fear of crippling his mount. It was then that he suddenly made out a solitary figure, on foot before him. With no weapon to hand, Tobias instinctively chose to ride him down and recklessly dug in his heels again. Then, at the last possible moment, he realized with a start that the stranger was a white man, and just managed to swerve aside.

As he pounded past with bare inches to spare, the teamster bellowed out the first thing that came into his head. 'They're torturing him up there!' And then he was gone, recklessly careering down the non-existent trail towards who knew what.

And sure enough, as the shod hoofs clattered away, Brad Dix could just make out some kind of unearthly wail coming through the gloom. 'The hell with this,' he muttered, unknowingly replicating Tobias's exact thoughts. Despite the chill air, he was sweating like a pig. In his case, extreme fear had always resulted in the production of various unpleasant fluids. Warily sniffing the air like an animal, he decided that by adding a little embellishment, he had now achieved more than enough to justify claiming Cope's one hundred dollar bonus. Thankfully turning away from the forbidding peaks, he slowly made his way back down towards his companions.

A short while later there came a flurry of shots and Dix affected a wolfish smile. That gunfire had to signify the fugitive's demise, which could only benefit him, because now there would not be anyone to contradict the gunhand's shaky grasp of the facts. Out of range of the screaming and now confident of his bonus, he began to feel a great deal happier. And then the memory of Perry Jakes' gruesome end flooded back, and he didn't want to be alone any more.

'You damned morons,' snarled Cope angrily, as he gazed down at the young man's bloodied features in the flickering light. His men had dragged the fresh corpse over near the small cooking fire that he had insisted on. 'You've killed one of Marsh's men.'

'So what?' retorted Jared Tiegs. 'It'll be one less for later, when we turn road agent.'

His employer was not mollified. 'I'm a scientist, not an outlaw. We're not here to *kill* Marsh and his people, just to frighten them into handing over the bones. This poor fellow might have had a wife and children.'

Tiegs tilted his head as he regarded Cope pityingly. In his opinion, it was high time that man adjusted to certain realities, because things had changed *and* they certainly weren't in Denver any more either. 'Happen you should have stayed back east where you belong, *Mister* Scientist. Did you really think that a man like Joe Eagle would just hand everything over to you without any killing, just because you'd bought yourself a few hired guns? That half-breed knocked seven shades of shit out of those two back at the railhead. Maybe you should have learnt from that.'

Cope didn't relish being spoken to in such a fashion and retaliated with bluster. 'Who the devil do you think you're talking to? I'm the man that's paying your wages.'

Before Tiegs could respond, everyone's attention was taken by a hail from the darkness. 'Don't shoot, for Christ's sake. It's me, Dix. I'm coming in.'

Moments later, that man appeared in the firelight, eyes wide and fearful as they took in the dead teamster. His relief at rejoining the others was obvious and certainly no act. 'Jesus, fellas. You could have kilt me as well.'

'Nah, we're not that dumb,' retorted Tiegs scornfully. 'That young fool came out of nowhere and he . . .'

'Never mind that,' Cope brusquely interrupted, keen to regain some control over the proceedings. 'What did you discover up there?'

Dix peered over at his employer, and everything seemed to come out in a rush. 'Hell's teeth, Mister Cope. That young fella that you done shot to pieces, visited with me on his way down here. Said those God-damned savages was torturing his buddies. And I heard the screams. It was something awful, like nothing I've ever heard before.'

'Huh, you obviously don't get out much,' Tiegs retorted, but Cope impatiently waved him to silence. 'You mean Marsh and all his men have been overrun by those heathens?'

The gunhand nodded vigorously. He was only half acting, because in truth it could quite easily be the case. All his tale needed was a little embellishment. 'That's what he done told me. Happen that's why he came at you so fast. He was scared to death . . . and now he is. Dead, that is.'

'But did you *see* any of this?'

This was where he had to be careful. 'No. No, I didn't, Mister Cope. Because truth is, I was scared to death myself. But unless it had been a white man screaming his lungs out, that boy wouldn't have been in such an all-fired hurry. It stands to reason.'

Cope nodded gravely. However reliable Dix might normally be, there could be no doubting the truth of

90

his story, because part of it lay dead by the fire. And he had had no hand in that. 'You've done well, Dix. The bonus will be yours. Get yourself a mug of coffee, while *I* decide what must be done.' He glared at Tiegs and the others, as though challenging them to oppose him, but they held their peace, because although loathe to admit it, Dix's words had genuinely affected them all.

It took the scientist some time to come to terms with the change of circumstances, because it appeared as though all his devious plans had come to nought. Thanks to his paid informant, he knew a great deal about Marsh's intentions, but not the most important part . . . the actual whereabouts of the dinosaur bones. Without that, and with no means of transporting them anyway, there was no point in going on. Which meant returning to Denver and then back east with his tail between his legs, like a whipped cur. Bitterly frustrated, he savagely kicked out at a stone. And yet what if this piece of frontier low life *had* genuinely got it wrong? There could still be a faint glimmer of hope. At least it would be something to clutch at for a while, before surrendering to humiliation.

Rounding on his employees, he abruptly announced his intentions. 'We're returning to the far side of Platte Canyon, where we'll remain until I say otherwise. There's water aplenty, and we've food enough for all. If this man is right, then we'll have just wasted some time. But if he isn't, and Marsh is still alive and finds those bones, then we'll still be able to relieve him of them on his way back. God knows, they surely won't be able to put up much resistance by then. Either way, you're all still on wages, so it'll make no difference to you. Agreed?'

It was Tiegs that spoke for the others, and there could be no disguising the relief in his voice. 'Can't argue with any of that, *Mister* Cope. After all, it's your money, and we sure as hell ain't got anything else to do at the minute!'

The terrible deed was done! Hayden's left arm was a shadow of its former self and the dreadfully tender stump had been cauterized with a red-hot blade. If anything, that had been the worst part of the whole disgusting business. The sweat-coated, haggard patient was drifting on the fringes of consciousness, his chances of survival anybody's guess. He had blacked out a number of times during the operation, but each time had come round. It had been as though his own body was torturing him. And yet, even then, when all he wanted was to be left alone, Joe hadn't quite finished with him. As the others looked on in amazement, he quite unexpectedly slapped Hayden sharply across the face.

'Now if you don't want me to start on the other arm,' he barked, 'you'd better tell me about your arrangement with Cope.'

Even a hardnose like Cartwright was stunned. 'For pity's sake, Joe. What are you about?'

That man ignored him and slapped Hayden's other cheek even harder. 'You hear me, you limp-dicked faggot? How much did he give you to sell us out?' As though to emphasize his intention, he waved his still bloodied Bowie in front of the assistant's face.

That was just too much for Cartwright. Drawing and cocking his revolver, he pointed it unwaveringly at Joe's head. 'Back off, Eagle,' he commanded, 'or face the consequences!'

Tom Hayden was oblivious to the sudden confrontation. He was aware of only two things: the sickening pain coursing through his body, and the huge knife in front of his eyes. At that moment in time, nothing else was relevant. 'Five hundred dollars!' he blurted out, raising his head from the rolled-up blanket. 'To tell him everything I knew. It was more money that I'd ever had in my life,' he added, as though that made it all acceptable.

Slowly nodding his head, Joe casually wiped his blade clean on Hayden's pants leg. Without even looking at Cartwright, he asked, 'You still gonna squeeze that trigger, Dave, or what?'

It was Marsh who replied. He had been in a state of shock throughout the whole amputation procedure, and was wondering just what more could happen. 'How did you know? I brought Tom with me from back east, and I never suspected him for one minute.'

Joe shrugged. 'That's because you were too close to him. It was easier for me, as I never liked him anyway. The teamsters were told very little, so it couldn't have been any of them. And since you weren't likely to sell yourself out, it had to be one of us four. It wasn't me, although land sakes I could use the money, and Ben wouldn't have been interested. All he's after is revenge. And since I've heard too many good things over the years about 'Buckskin' Dave, that only left this son of a bitch.'

Sheathing his knife, Joe clambered to his feet, but he hadn't quite finished. Gazing down at Hayden, he coldly remarked, 'I've done the best I can with that arm. Whether you live or die now is up to you, but either way I don't really give a damn!'

The Anasazi chief was sorely troubled by the capabilities of these intruders. Their weapons possessed great power and they used them with ruthless skill. But that was only the half of it! What really disturbed him was the fact that they seemed to derive strange pleasure from torturing their own kind. They must surely obtain some form of strength from their victim by doing so, but any people with the capacity for such behaviour deserved only complete annihilation . . . and yet that task was not proving easy.

As he squatted in the darkness on a ledge overlooking the camp, the chief came to a decision. That day's attack had cost the lives of far too many of his warriors. There would be no more head-on assaults. From now on the Anasazi would utilize the mountains themselves against the white invaders. With their naturally superior speed and agility, they would pick them off one by one. Since they had come with the intention of stealing the sacred bones, it was only right that theirs should end up bleached by the sun in the very same basin!

*

Yet another new day had dawned, the sixth, but it was quite likely that none of the group could have said with certainty just how long it was since they had left Denver. They had too much else to think about. With the loss of three teamsters, the task of leading the remaining fifteen mules had been spread across everyone, with the exception of Hayden and their scout. Marsh's erstwhile assistant should really have been confined to bed, but to have left him behind would have constituted a death sentence, so his ankles had been roped together under the horse that he had inherited from one of the dead men. Feverish and mostly oblivious to their progress, he swayed to and fro in his saddle as the expedition moved ever higher into the mountains.

One thing of consequence to the whole group happened that morning. They finally and very reluctantly bade farewell to the South Platte river, as that watercourse curved away towards the north-west. From now on they would have to rely on their canteens and any springs that they encountered. And that wasn't the only sobering occurrence.

From his position as 'point' man, Joe gazed along the full length of the steep defile ahead, and his heart sank. This was Platte Canyon all over again, albeit on a much smaller scale. As Ben Mudge joined him, Joe remarked, 'There could be any number of those sons of bitches up there, waiting on us to pass, and there probably is. Because they always seem to know where we're at.'

Mudge nodded glumly. 'They've permanently got the advantage of higher ground. It wouldn't surprise me if one of the bastards weren't clinging to the sides of one of those peaks. You could see the whole dang world from up there. It's just a shame you ain't a real eagle, 'cause if'n you were, you could go up and get him.'

Joe stared at him wide-eyed for a moment. That had given him something to think about, but it would have to wait until later . . . after they had got through the damned ravine. Because if he wasn't careful, there was a very strong chance that none of them would!

'What do you think, Joe?' For Othniel Marsh, that sort of question was now quite natural, because he had no doubt that without the services of the Cherokee scout the expedition would not be where it was. The only thing that continued to niggle was the appalling loss of life involved.

'I think we're gonna have to ride hard and fast. One man at a time, with the animals that are assigned to him. Those cockchafers'll make a play, but I don't think they'll try to block the pass this time, because it didn't work before. I reckon they'll heave rocks down without showing themselves, and try to pick some of us off.' Raising his voice, he added, 'I'm going through first with Hayden. Then I'll cover you all from the far end. If you see anything moving up there at all, get to shooting.' With that, he took a tight hold on the injured man's reins and dug his heels in.

'Here we go again,' Cartwright muttered, as he readied his Winchester. There was no visible movement on the ravine's edges, but of course that didn't mean a damn thing . . . as they were about to find out.

Joe and his barely conscious companion were pounding through the narrow gap when the first projectile came down. A rock the size of a generous melon struck the ground just behind the rear horse, rapidly followed by more of the same.

'Open fire,' Cartwright bellowed, but in truth there was no one to shoot at. The Anasazi had learnt a great deal of respect for the expedition's guns. They were keeping well back from the rim and hurling their missiles blind. It would be pure luck whether any of the white men were struck.

Suddenly, unbelievably, Joe and Hayden were through untouched. Dropping to the hard ground, the scout tethered both sets of reins under a heavy rock, and took a quick look around. A stunning vista stretched ahead of him, dominated by the snow-capped mountain known as Pikes Peak. They were well and truly up in the Rampart Range, and as he had expected there wasn't an Indian in sight. They were too busy throwing stones!

'Come on,' he yelled back. 'Ride like the devil and don't look up.'

As the next rider, a teamster with four mules, burst into motion, more rocks came flying over the rim, and Joe suddenly glimpsed a human form. Rapidly drawing a bead, he fired, levered in another cartridge and fired again. His victim stumbled uncontrollably towards the edge, where more bullets struck him, and then tumbled down the steep side of the ravine. Three things then happened pretty much at once. As the teamster reached the far side unhurt, his companions broke into a ragged cheer, and the dead warrior's broken form finally came to rest by the side of the non-existent trail.

Next across was Ben Mudge, and he had no problem at all. Apparently hesitant after suffering another casualty, the Anasazi maintained only a desultory bombardment. The same was true for Marsh, who also crossed unhindered. Then, without any audible reproaches from above, everything changed. A volley of missiles came cascading over the rim, just as the other remaining teamster surged forwards. For no apparent reason, one of his mules suddenly turned ornery, acting as a drag on the main group. Sadly, it paid for its cussedness with its life, because a sizeable rock plummeted down, crushing the poor creature's skull. The animal dropped to the ground as though pole-axed, nearly dragging the teamster with it. By necessarily relinquishing the reins for one, so he did for all and abruptly there was chaos.

Three mules were free to choose their own course, which due to their contrary natures had to be the wrong one. As Dave Cartwright watched the three beasts turn back towards him, he knew that he had no chance of catching them, whilst still controlling his own animals. That only left him with one option.

'Shit in a bucket,' he muttered. 'Marsh ain't gonna like this.'

Swiftly levelling his Winchester for an awkward one-handed shot, he fired at the nearest hairy asset. It was close range and his hurried aim was true. With blood spurting from its neck, the mule's front legs buckled and it collapsed across the trail. The other two reared up before it and promptly reversed direction.

Leading his own beasts over the twitching carcass, Cartwright swept through the ravine. With five Winchesters now crashing out a concentrated fire at the far end, the number of missiles diminished and he and all the remaining animals made it safely. Reining in next to his employer, he gestured back towards the mule that he had just shot. 'Right sorry about that, Mister Marsh, but it was kill one to save two.'

The scientist was on the point of responding, when Ben Mudge uttered two horrified words that altered everything: 'Where's Hayden?'

A sense of shock and disbelief settled over all six men as they peered around. It wasn't long before their worst fears were confirmed. A short distance away, the assistant's horse lay on its side in a pool of blood. Its throat had been torn open. Of Tom Hayden there was no sign. It was as though he had disappeared into thin air, although as Cartwright pointed out it was far more likely that he had been carried off, to be utilized as a source of sick entertainment by his captors.

99

'It don't look like those bastards put much store by Winchesters,' he added, glancing at the full scabbard on the dead animal. 'Which is mighty lucky for us, because if they did we'd be between a rock and a hard place, an' that's a fact.'

CHAPTER EIGHT

The screaming began just as the last vestiges of light drained out of the sky, and suddenly it was shaping up to be a long, cold night in more senses than one. As the horrific cries continued without let up, seemingly echoing around their camp, a white-faced Othniel Marsh stared at the expedition's scout.

'What does this mean, Joe?'

The other man shrugged. He'd received more intelligent questions in his life. 'I reckon they're out to prove that they're better at that sort of thing than we are . . . and because they know that the noise will work on our nerves. Like as not, those sons of bitches'll be skinning him. Because you're not the only bone collector in these mountains, *Mister* Scientist!'

'Oh dear God! What can we do?'

Joe, very conscious that the others were listening, remained silent, but Marsh persisted. 'There must be *something* we can do!'

Joe sighed. 'To save him, nothing. He's as good as dead. But to save ourselves, maybe.' Then, as the five

101

remaining members of the expedition drew closer, he began to elaborate. 'Ben gave me the idea earlier today. Those dirt worshippers always have the edge, because they seem to know exactly where we are every step of the way. We've lost four men and seven mules already. If this keeps up, none of us will see Denver again, with or without the bones you came for.' He paused and gestured towards the dark, looming bulk of the mountain behind them. 'I reckon their headman uses Pike's Peak as a lookout point and signals our whereabouts to his warriors. If I can get up there and kill him, they'll have lost their edge, and maybe a bit of spirit as well. And it has to be done tomorrow, because according to Ben there's a deep ravine ahead that cuts across our route and can only be crossed in single file. So if ever they intend to hit us in force again, that has to be the place.'

Marsh opened his mouth to respond, but Joe hadn't quite finished, and not for the first time that trip, brusquely cut him off. 'But I ain't doing it for free. No, siree. I didn't sign on as an assassin, and certainly not as a mountain climber. So it's gonna cost you an extra two hundred gold simoleons.'

His employer was stunned. 'That's outrageous. Apart from the fact that I'm not made of money, you have already contracted to take us all to the bone site and then back to Denver.'

Joe was completely unmoved by that argument. 'Damn right we have a contract, but there are no bones up there on Pike's Peak, and there *is* a very fair chance that I won't survive the climb. So for that I want two hundred dollars American. If you ain't up to paying it, then this trip's as good as over. Ask Cartwright. He'll tell you.' With that, he simply turned and walked away, over to where the animals had been tethered and hobbled for the night.

Marsh stared after his retreating figure with great distaste. Underneath his voluminous facial hair, his teeth began to grind together, as they usually did when he became really angry or upset. Even his assistant's continued screams were temporarily pushed to the back of his mind. 'God damn the man,' he muttered, and then was abruptly aware that 'Buckskin' Dave was at his side.

'Eagle's got you between a rock and a hard place,' that man opined.

'But there ain't no getting away from the fact that he's right . . . as usual. We can't keep taking casualties, either man or beast, so unless we can get those heathens off our backs, this expedition really will be over. And all that cash money you've spent so far will have gone to waste.'

Marsh stared at him in silence for a while as he tried to get a grip on his emotions. Deep down, he knew that what Cartwright said was true, and Hayden's continued and very audible anguish only supported the fact – but it was still a bitter pill to swallow. 'Very well, I'll agree to his terms,' he eventually blurted out. 'But you'll have to tell him. I can't face the scoundrel right now. He's very adept at stripping away a man's illusions.'

Cartwright grunted understandingly, but he hadn't quite finished. 'I ain't right sure what that last bit meant, but I will say this. He might be a robbing bastard, but he's no scoundrel, because I wouldn't go up that mountain after some axe-wielding maniac for any amount of money!'

The two men sat quietly in the dark, watching and listening. It had been some time since Hayden's last agonised wail, and the decreased volume had been very noticeable.

'Reckon he's dead?' Cartwright queried softly.

'Happen so. A body can only stand so much, and he wasn't used to roughing it. Heart probably gave out.'

They were quiet again for a while, until Cartwright posed a question on a subject that had been bugging him for days. He knew that with Joe soon to depart, he might well not get another chance. 'Mind if I ask you something?'

It was as though the scout had read his thoughts. 'Get it in while you can, huh?' He chuckled. 'Yeah, yeah, ask away.'

'What is it with you and money? You don't look like a cardsharp or a high roller, so what's this desperate need for the stuff?'

Joe Eagle's eyes glinted in the moonlight as he turned to regard his companion. He stared at him for a long while, before finally answering: 'You remember back in Denver, in the hotel, when you *tested* me? I told you I was one-eighth Cherokee. Well,

104

that's true. I am. I have kin still living that survived the Trail of Tears. They passed on tales of terrible suffering that don't bear thinking on – the sort of stories that burn into a youngster's brain. Whatever else history says about that President van Buren, he was a bastard for bringing all that about. The Cherokee are some of the finest folks that you could hope to meet, but they and their kind are living in poverty, starving to death, in the so-called Indian Territories. Their numbers drop every year, but nobody seems to give a damn.'

'Except you?'

Joe nodded. 'Except me. Whenever I get hold of some *dinero*, they get a share. So if I survive this trip, and it's a big if, they're gonna get some of the money that that porky scientist's brought out west with him. It's the least I can do to help.'

Cartwright frowned. 'He's really not a bad man, you know. You don't always have to treat him like shit.'

Joe shrugged. His lack of interest was obvious. 'He doesn't belong out here, is all.' And then, abruptly, that particular conversation was over. Rising to his feet, he slung the Winchester diagonally across his back and then broke the sawn-off to check its cartridges. His intention was to be clear of the camp and on the mountain itself before daybreak. It was time to make a move. Briefly returning his attention to Cartwright, he gave him some last-minute instructions:

'Whatever happens to me, your best bet is to give

105

Mudge his head. He might still be hurting inside, but he seems like a good man and he knows the way to the basin. And remember, don't be in any all-fired hurry to set off come daylight. Your dawdlin' around should puzzle them and maybe keep their attention off me. I need to kill whoever's up there before he can organize any more ambushes for you.'

Cartwright nodded and abruptly thrust out his right hand. 'For what it's worth, I wish you well . . . for all our sakes. And I hope those Cherokees come into some money, 'cause happen they deserve it.'

Joe Eagle, one-eighth Cherokee, briefly accepted his strong grip, and then he was gone.

Dawn's first rays of light were barely registering in the sky, but the Anasazi chief was already back on 'Heey-otoyoo', as it was known by the Arapaho Indians. Although not of their tribe, he approved of the name, as 'Long Mountain' seemed a fitting description. The chief was making for a barely accessible eyrie from which he would be able to observe both the intruders' current campsite and their expected route. He knew full well that another day's travel would see them at the sacred basin, and that event had to be prevented at all costs, even if it meant another costly all-out assault, because he simply could not allow the bones of the ancients to fall into the hands of unbelievers. It was a sad fact that the closer the 'white eyes' got, the more desperate he became. So much so that his anxiety was beginning to affect his normally sound judgement.

Confronted by a nearly sheer rock face, he began to climb with barely a pause. His fingers and toes seemed to almost instinctively find the small openings that were all he needed to carry him ever higher. And then, after a seemingly effortless climb, he arrived in a small alcove that afforded some slight shelter from the relentless wind that had picked up. Below him stretched a heart-stopping drop that few men in their right minds would contemplate tackling.

His sharp eyes easily picked out the intruders far below, and bafflingly they had not yet broken camp. Always before, they had been on the move shortly after first light – but not this time. He was aware of his warriors dotted around awaiting his instructions, but he had none to give them. Perhaps one of the white men was ill, or maybe they were running scared and finally contemplating withdrawal. The Anasaza smiled grimly. The very audible punishment that his men had inflicted on their prisoner during the dark hours could well have broken their spirit.

Then, after what seemed an age, the six remaining white men and their pack animals set off on what would have to be their final day alive. Leaning precariously out of his rudimentary refuge, the chief began to point and signal to specific warriors. He well knew that before the sun had arced much further across the sky, their enemies would reach the deep ravine that could only be traversed by way of a natural bridge of remarkably resilient rock that had been in place for aeons. It was here that they would be most vulnerable, and it was here that they would all die!

As the six members of Marsh's expedition set off, Cartwright's lips crinkled into a smile as he watched their scout jiggle about on the back of a mule. The wooden-framed construction that they had put together during the night had been strapped to the back of the animal, and then the hat and bloodied jacket that Joe had recovered from the dead teamster had been added as a finishing touch. All of which showed that their absent companion didn't miss a trick.

'The new Joe Eagle is certainly less trouble than the old one,' Cartwright joked, in an attempt to prod the others out of their gloomy mood. Hayden's awful fate had affected them more deeply than they cared to admit, because they all knew it could quite easily have been one of them. 'It's amazing how he shrugged off an axe in the back the way he did,' he persisted. 'Don't you think? Huh, huh?'

His employer finally glanced his way, favouring him with a weak smile. 'Your exuberance is to be commended, Dave. I just hope that no one discovers this little ruse. At least not for a while.'

'That's why we need to keep those cockchafers at a distance,' that man replied, all traces of humour abruptly gone. Raising his voice, he added, 'Anything moves out there, blast it!' And then instinctively his eyes moved towards Pike's Peak. 'Rather him than me,' he muttered.

*

With a coil of rope and an arsenal of weapons, Joe was carrying far more than he would ideally have wished for. Unfortunately, surrounded as he was by hostiles, it really wasn't possible to travel light. Having securely tethered his horse to a tree branch, he was now climbing on foot, each step taking him further up the mountainside. He clutched the sawn-off in both hands, but recognized that pretty soon he would need them for sourcing handholds.

He paused for a moment to scrutinize his surroundings. The air was crystal clear, the landscape stunning, and he reflected that it was just a pure shame that people were trying to kill each other in such an environment. It was no wonder that the old-style mountain men had been drawn to these remote areas, although as ever, money in the form of furs had had something to do with the attraction as well.

He was not yet sufficiently high enough to make out his companions, but he knew their rough position and consequently had a fair idea where the 'spy in the sky' was likely to be. Because, to someone unused to the Rockies, the sky seemed to be where he was heading!

As his legs propelled him ever higher, he was aware of the warm sun on his back. And yet he didn't feel hot, only slightly breathless. The air was getting thinner with every step, and he knew that put him at a disadvantage against the man he was hunting. Time and again he checked his back trail far below, but there was no sign that he had been discovered. And then, suddenly, the only way was straight up. With both long guns now slung across his back, he was uncomfortably defenceless. And, as he carefully identified tenuous handholds, it occurred to him that getting down would be a whole lot harder. His coil of rope, although long, would be nowhere near enough, and even using that depended on there being something to anchor it to.

Up and up he went. Beads of sweat formed on his face, as much from discomfort as exertion. To his jaundiced eye, the upper reaches of Pike's Peak appeared to consist solely of unbroken, vertical rock, but of course that wasn't true at all. There were plenty of minor crevices and outcrops where he could find hand- and footholds. He just wasn't used to that kind of activity.

Grazing his left hand against one such small outcrop, Joe cursed softly and paused to assess his situation. Looking down, he could now make out the expedition as it wended slowly towards the ravine. On its periphery, he also spotted a number of Anasazi as they dogged their prey. Joe felt an instinctive urge to bellow down a warning, but of course that just wouldn't do.

Swivelling his head around, he peered up and to his left, towards where he expected to see their leader. Nothing. Not a damn thing. Sighing with disappointment, he recommenced climbing. Struggling ever higher, he began to lose track of time. Everything focused on finding the next handholds.

Then his moist fingers slipped out of a tiny crevice, and his body slammed painfully against the rock face. With blood suddenly streaming from a cut on his face, Joe began to feel the stirrings of panic.

'Get a grip,' he snarled angrily, but he couldn't shake the growing fear of being trapped on the mountain. With little experience of serious climbing, he was out of his element, and knew it. Forcing himself to draw in some deep breaths, he resisted the nagging urge to glance down. That would most certainly do him no good at all. Instead, the very reluctant mountaineer looked up, desperately searching for some sign, any sign of his quarry. Unbelievably, there was still nothing.

'This can't be,' he muttered miserably. Then, about fifty feet above and to his left, a long brown arm suddenly swept out in an arc, as though urging watching men to sweep around someone's flank. 'Got him,' he announced triumphantly, if a little prematurely. But leastways he did now know where the bastard was.

The shock, as some object struck rock a few feet away, nearly pitched him clean off Pike's Peak. Uncomprehendingly, he twisted his head from side to side, but there was simply nothing to see. Then another missile slammed into the mountain directly above him, and this time he heard the shot.

'Sweet Jesus,' he exclaimed. 'Someone's shooting at me!'

A moment later, yet another bullet ricocheted off the rock face, this time well below him, and his befuddled mind suddenly grasped what was happening. The Anasazi were using some kind of single-shot rifle against him. Then it came to him. Joe Leidy's 'trapdoor' Springfield! Someone in the tribe had finally got around to experimenting with a captured firearm. The only saving grace was that it wasn't one of Oliver Winchester's marvellous creations.

Although it was often a fallacy to claim that Indians 'couldn't shoot worth a damn', the carbine's powerful recoil and their undoubted ignorance of guns explained why the shots were all over the place. Yet they had achieved one thing. Their leader now knew that he was being hunted, although that situation could quite possibly end up being reversed.

The next shot was uncomfortably close, with chips of rock painfully scoring his cheek. He now had blood streaming down both sides of his face. It was definitely time to shift position, if only because a moving target was harder to hit. But where to go? He couldn't make directly for the chief, because that individual must surely be waiting for him, and yet returning to terra firma was now also out of the question. It was one of the very rare moments in Joe Eagle's life when he really wasn't sure what to do next.

'Who the hell's doing that shooting?' Cartwright demanded. He peered around at his four companions, but no one had been hit. It was Ben Mudge who supplied the sobering answer, and its implications were frightening: 'Those devils are using Joe Leidy's carbine. They must be shooting at Joe!'

The five men had been cautiously shepherding the remaining mules towards the ravine, so far unhindered by any aggression. Now they reined in, all eyes on Pike's Peak. Initially they struggled to spot Joe Eagle, in part because he was deliberately wearing neutral-coloured clothing. Then another shot crashed out, and dust kicked up on the face near a struggling figure.

'Shit in a bucket,' Cartwright exclaimed. 'Those cockchafers'll have him for sure.'

It was Othniel Marsh who highlighted their dilemma. 'It wasn't his intention, but it turns out he's distracting those savages. We could slip across that ravine and make for the bone fields – but what will become of him?'

'Dead as a wagon tyre, for sure,' Mudge opined. 'But I'm not gonna let that happen. I've already left one good man up in these mountains. *His* cries in the night will live with me for the rest of my life. So you folks keep moving. I'm for getting that Springfield back!'

Before Marsh could respond, Cartwright emphatically shook his head. 'That won't answer. You know the exact location of those bones, and I'm far better with a gun than you. So the answer's obvious. You lead the others the rest of the way, whilst Joe Eagle and I rescue Joe Eagle.'

The others stared at him in total bewilderment, until with a grin he pointed at the wooden-framed horseman. 'You couldn't recruit much more of a stiff than him, so he can be my ace in the hole.'

Marsh appeared to be torn by indecision, but there simply wasn't time for that. As though piling on the pressure, strange shrieks began to echo around Pike's Peak. They could only belong to the individual that Joe had gone after, and reinforced the fact that any possibility of surprise was long gone.

'I ain't debating this,' Cartwright continued forcefully. 'We need to make our move *now*, or Joe's a dead man and we all get swamped crossing that ravine!' With that, he seized the reins belonging to his decoy's mule and pulled away from the others.

Taking his cue from 'Buckskin' Dave, Mudge gave the order, 'Follow me!' and promptly set off leading his quota of pack animals.

Although shaking his head in dismay, Marsh had no choice other than to follow on with the two teamsters. As the ever-dwindling expedition moved off to the south, each of its four remaining members wondered if they would ever see Dave Cartwright and Joe Eagle again. Part of their concern was due in no small measure to self interest, because they all knew that without those two men they had little chance of ever seeing Denver again, either!

CHAPTER NINE

For the first time in his life, Joe Eagle seriously wished that he could emulate his namesake. Bullet after bullet continued to smack into the rock face around him, and his only ally appeared to be the Anasazi's appalling accuracy. Their chief howled unintelligible insults at him, but seemed disinclined to pursue him across the mountain while his warrior was taking pot-shots with the captured carbine. As another near miss spat stone chips at him, Joe grimly accepted that somehow he had to make a move.

Desperately, he craned his neck in search of succour. And then he saw it: directly above him, some sixty or seventy feet away, a single stunted limber pine tree grew out of a fissure in the rock. If he could reach that and tie his rope end to it, he might be able to swing over to a spot just above the Anasazi chief's refuge. From there, with his selection of firearms, he should easily be able to slay him. Even so, there were a hell of a lot of 'ifs, buts and maybes' involved – *and* he was still under fire from that damned Springfield.

'Oh shit, come on you lazy bastard,' he snarled, and with that impetus reached up in search of his next handhold. Higher and higher he climbed, occasionally slipping but never stopping, and all the time harried by that cursed carbine. Then, just as his left hand was on the point of closing on a tiny outcrop, a bullet struck the base of his little finger and sheared it clean off. Overwhelming pain exploded up his arm and seemed to spurt into the base of his skull. Crying out in his terrible distress, Joe's every instinct was to cradle the injured extremity in his other hand, but such an action would surely see him plummeting to his death. And then, as though by some deliberately twisted design, yet another piece of lead flattened out between his legs, barely an inch below his crotch, and he suddenly knew with great certainty that the next one would kill him!

Much to his surprise, 'Buckskin' Dave was able to close in on the base of Pike's Peak without being discovered. Then he realized why: Joe Eagle was doing his job too well for his own good. High up the mountainside, the Anasazi chief was preoccupied with the lone white man's progress, whilst his warriors were mesmerized by their own inept attempts to shoot him down. Then one of their bullets finally did some real damage.

Cartwright watched with dismay as the scout's left hand jerked off the rock face. Despite the distance, it was clear that he was in terrible pain. The Indian possessing the carbine briefly celebrated with a gleeful

howl, before returning to his task of knocking the
hated intruder clear off *their* mountain. Clumsily
closing the 'trapdoor' over a fresh cartridge, he took
aim and fired yet again. The horrified observer knew
that he had to act fast.

Releasing his hold on the decoy's mule, Cartwright
rapidly drew a bead on the animal's rump and fired.
The bullet tore a bloody furrow through the poor
beast's flesh, causing it to buck wildly in agony and
then gallop headlong towards the closely packed
group of warriors. Caught completely unawares, they
didn't even have the chance to scatter. The pain-mad-
dened creature wanted only to escape the source of
its distress, and so rather than avoiding the Indians,
ploughed straight into them. Bodies knocked to the
hard ground were then trampled by iron-hard hoofs.
Those warriors on the periphery were initially taken
in by the swaying wooden frame, and so considered
the rider to be the main foe. They were soon to be
otherwise enlightened.

Keeping just beyond reach of the main throng,
and yet still at lethally close range, Cartwright levelled his Winchester and opened fire. Short of maybe
a highly unwieldy Gatling gun, there was no finer
repeating weapon in existence, and his carbine
wrought terrible destruction. By design, his first
bullet killed the owner of the Springfield, thereby
immediately taking the pressure off Joe Eagle. After
that, working the lever action with controlled ferocity, he simply fired indiscriminately at those beyond
reach of the frenzied mule. With seventy-five grains

of black powder igniting behind each bullet, they truly were man-stoppers.

The Anasazi, their flesh punctured and limbs shattered, reeled before his savage onslaught. No mere mortals, armed only with primitive weapons, could withstand that kind of assault for long. Unable to comprehend that they were actually only up against one man, those that could, fled. Their assailant lined up a last shot at the rearmost warrior, and with a smile of satisfaction squeezed the trigger. A dull metallic click was his only reward.

'You lucky bastard,' he muttered, and rapidly began to feed fresh cartridges into the loading gate of the empty weapon.

Then, as yet another of Marsh's four-legged assets also unavoidably disappeared from view, Cartwright rode into the centre of the carnage and dismounted. After calmly placing a bullet into each and every one of the groaning wounded, he recovered the Springfield. Having no desire to either use it or carry it, he smashed its action against a rock until it was totally inoperative. Only then did he glance up at the giddily distant figure of Joe Eagle.

That man appeared to be struggling with his left hand, but there was little to be gained in attempting to shout up to him. So next, Cartwright peered over at the Anasazi chief's refuge. Tucking the carbine's butt tightly into his shoulder, he momentarily took aim, before sadly accepting that he didn't have a hope in hell of hitting anything. Even with a full-length rifle barrel, he would have had no chance of placing a bullet *inside* the refuge. Because of the angle, he couldn't even see beyond the outcrop at the base of it.

Temporary and very unaccustomed indecision assailed him, until he determined there was little else he could contribute. Strangely, it never occurred to him that his presence might be sufficient to keep the chief bottled up and therefore an easier target for Joe. Dave Cartwright was a man to whom inactivity did not sit well. Better by far to ride off in support of those to whom killing folks came less easy. All of which meant that, rightly or wrongly, Joe was on his own . . . for now. And so, after a wry glance at the decoy's shattered framework, 'Buckskin' Dave swung his horse away, all the while hoping that the real Joe Eagle did not end up like that!

As the momentary light-headedness passed, Joe became aware of an outbreak of rapid firing far below and his spirits soared. Unless the Anasazi had captured a Winchester, it appeared as though someone had come to his aid. And sure enough, the sniping against him abruptly stopped. But none of that altered his precarious position on the peak. The pain from his bloodied stump was almost heart-stopping in its intensity.

With his face pressed against solid rock, Joe first tested the footholds before using his right hand to awkwardly unfasten his neckerchief. Literally crying with pain and frustration, it was some time before he managed it. Then, with an unremitting wind tugging

119

at his body, he stretched both hands above his head and clumsily bound the wound as tightly as he could bear. Tears and snot poured over his already blood-ied features, as by touch alone he finally tucked one end into the folds. At last he was ready to continue climbing. And with the lone tree beckoning, he did exactly that.

Every time he used his left hand, the pain was excruciating, but bit by bit he closed in. A rapid glance over at the Anasazi's alcove confirmed that that man was remaining hidden, and Joe's spirits began to recover. He struck out with renewed vigour, and quite suddenly he was there. The crevice, with its single natural growth, was actually agreeably larger than it had appeared from below. It possessed a narrow, slightly sloping ledge that would allow the amateur climber the chance of a respite from the gruelling demands of the almost sheer face.

But as he crouched there clinging on to the almost horizontal pine tree, Joe made the mistake of gazing down on his starting point. The terrifying drop caused his heart to miss a beat and he quickly looked away. He couldn't even begin to contemplate his eventual descent, and so instead switched all his efforts on to securing one end of his coil of rope to the tree. It was as he struggled to achieve this that a sudden movement registered on his peripheral vision.

All the while consumed by impotent rage, the chief had helplessly viewed the one-sided slaughter far below. It belatedly occurred to him that perhaps they should have embraced the white man's weaponry, but until this latest incursion there had simply been no need. The strange ones had nothing that his people wanted, and probably hadn't even known of the Anasazi's existence until they discovered the sacred relics. That had changed everything, and unless he acted fast, many of the bones would be stolen and taken far away from the mountain stronghold.

He was confident that his surviving warriors would continue to harass the expedition, but without his overall control they would struggle to stop it. And if he was to regain his influence, the chief first had to dispose of the lone climber. Cautiously peering out of his rocky alcove, he looked first to his left and then up. Amazingly, the wounded yet stubbornly determined assassin had reached the crevice above his position, and now appeared to be anchoring a rope. If the Anasazi was to make a move, it would have to be immediately.

He didn't bother to check on the situation below. Even if there was a white man down there with a fire stick, the chief would be moving far too quickly. And so, safe in the certain knowledge that he was faster than his pursuer would ever live to be, he swung sideways off the ledge and moved across the rock face as though he had been born to it!

'It's a miracle,' Othniel Marsh yelled jubilantly.

The expedition had crossed the ravine without

loss, with only a few stones hurled at them from too great a distance to cause any damage. Now, according to a rather pensive Ben Mudge, they were finally within spitting distance of the bone fields.

'Well, if it is, it's a 45/75 miracle with plenty of guts behind it,' retorted Cartwright, as he came up behind them. 'I've thinned those bastards out a bit more, an' hopefully Joe will parole that poxy chief to Jesus.'

He had barely spoken before the five men and their now invaluable twelve mules reached the crest of the steep rocky slope that led down to the vast basin. Quite suddenly, the immense quantity of 'bone treasure' lay before them for the taking. The awe-inspiring 'field' of dinosaur relics was everything that Marsh had imagined it to be, and more. Sadly, though unsurprisingly, Joe Eagle's fate no longer had any place in the scientist's thoughts.

'Oh, my God,' he exclaimed. 'Will you look at that?' His fleshy, hairy features expressed the sheer wonder that he felt at their discovery. Glancing over at Mudge, he added, 'Everything you told me was true.'

His field collector's expression was rather harder to read. '*I* never doubted it for a moment,' he retorted sharply, but such ire was completely lost on his preoccupied employer.

That man was already urging his horse down the slope at breakneck speed. 'Come on, come on,' he impatiently hollered back at the teamsters. 'Get those mules down here. We've got so much to do.'

Those men followed on, but with far less enthusiasm. Three of their number were either dead or gone, and yet the really hard work that they were being paid for was only just about to begin.

Cartwright and Mudge came up in the rear, their eyes roving over the bruising landscape. Then, as they reached the smooth basin, the latter reined in, his eyes wide with shock as he stared at the remains of an old campfire. 'My God, that was ours. You can even see Joe Leidy's blood.'

Sure enough, the blackened embers remained from that horrific night, and close by, the sun-baked bloodstains. The sobering sight served as a reminder, if one were even needed, that they, too, were not alone in the mountains.

Cartwright instinctively glanced up at Pike's Peak. He was beginning to feel pangs of guilt at leaving Joe Eagle to his fate. Then Marsh's excited, almost child-like cries intruded, and he came to a decision. Dismounting, he carefully walked over to join his employer. That man was measuring and listing those specimens nearest to him with every appearance of great joy. But what 'Buckskin' Dave had to say was guaranteed to take some of the wind out of his sails.

'We ain't spending more than one night here, Mister Marsh. I don't reckon those sons of bitches will try anything again in daylight. There's too much open ground hereabouts for them to rush us, what with us toting these Winchesters an' all. But come night time . . . well, Ben here knows all about that.'

Mudge nodded grimly. 'Damn right I do. What we

123

need then is a big fire between us and that broken ground. That way we'll get plenty of time to see them and shoot, before they get close enough to use those God-damn spears. So me, I'm gonna start collecting wood.'

Marsh blinked rapidly as he absorbed that exchange. He was finally in his element and didn't relish the distraction, but some of their words *had* sunk in. It was certainly true that he had experienced more than enough bloodshed for one lifetime. And so, turning to Cartwright, he remarked with rather too much pomposity, 'I accept that under the circumstances we cannot dally here for as long as I would have liked. And since that is the case, you'll have to double as a teamster and start packing some of these bones . . . under my direction, of course.'

The seasoned frontiersman surveyed him silently for a moment, as he chose his words carefully. 'Apart from the fact that I don't do that kind of work, I've got more pressing business to attend to. Joe Eagle's atop that mountain somewhere, wounded and hurting and hunting down that Anasazi lookout . . . for *you.* If he should manage to make it down off of there, he's gonna need help, and I aim to be there.' With that, he turned away and began to lead his horse back towards the edge of the basin.

Othniel Marsh, now seriously annoyed at the interruption to his work, wasn't about to tolerate any more insubordination. It had been bad enough having to compromise so much with that damned Eagle fellow. 'Don't you turn your back on me, Mister

Cartwright,' he barked out. 'This is my expedition and I pay your wages, remember?'

His employee paused and glanced back at him, which emboldened the scientist to go a little further than he perhaps should have. 'That's right. You'd do well to listen to me for a change, because I'll tell you this. If you walk away from here without my permission, I'll see to it that you never get employment again . . . with anyone. Do I make myself clear?'

Absorbing the rather ridiculous threat, Cartwright's jaw tightened almost imperceptibly. Then, as he scrutinized his boss, his eyes turned to chips of ice, but nevertheless he slowly retraced his steps. Finally, as the two men stood face to face, he emitted a deep sigh and softly uttered two words: 'Very clear!'

At that point, Marsh should have backed off, and fast, but there were still times when he really didn't possess the sense that he'd been born with.

CHAPTER TEN

With the rope finally secure and hanging vertically beneath his position, Joe breathed a great sigh of relief. It was time to take a much-needed respite. His left hand was throbbing abominably, but at least he had a temporary base from which to strike out at his prey. Given his height advantage and the benefit of a rope, it should be relatively easy to clamber down at an angle until he was above the Anasazi's refuge. But all that could wait, at least for a few moments while he rested his aching limbs. Twisting sideways, he eased his backside on to the gently sloping rock in the crevice and apprehensively glanced down.

The seemingly sheer drop alone was enough to send a shiver up his spine, but that was suddenly the least of his worries: the Indian lookout, apparently unconcerned by Joe's firearms, had unexpectedly left his eyrie, and was on the move ... directly towards the wide-eyed scout. He was climbing up across the rock face with unbelievable speed and catlike grace – it was almost as though he were moving horizontally.

His opponent's matchless agility sent a jolt of raw fear through Joe, who reacted in the only way possible. And yet, even as he drew and cocked his revolver, a much better idea came to him. This particular Anasazi hadn't yet experienced the terrifying power of a double-barrelled shotgun, which meant that he couldn't possibly know of its wide spread of shot. And only the fact that Joe was wedged in the fissure allowed him such an opportunity to use the heavy weapon.

Abruptly holstering his Schofield, he swung the sawn-off off his back and retracted both hammers. The Indian, who had narrowed the gap to around twenty-five yards, glanced up and across just as the big gun's gaping muzzles poked over the edge in his direction. Anticipating one or maybe two pieces of lead coming his way, he literally leapt to one side and with almost superhuman ability located two more handholds whilst he was still in motion. His probing fingers had just made contact when Joe triggered the twelve-gauge.

The jarring recoil across the scout's injured hand brought fresh tears to his eyes, but he couldn't allow himself the luxury of any distractions. As a great cloud of powder smoke was whisked away on the wind, he eagerly peered down to see what damage he had caused. The wide spread pattern had not claimed his enemy's life, but that man had definitely not escaped unscathed.

Two pellets had torn bloody furrows into the

Anasazi's right leg, with one of them lodging in the great thigh muscle. A tremendous spasm swept through the limb that almost broke his tenuous grip. Snarling from a mixture of pain and rage, the chief flexed his injured, bleeding leg and immediately realized that it could not take the strain of a rapid ascent. And yet, seeing that his foe had drawn another weapon, he knew that he had to do *something*. Glancing to his right, he suddenly knew what that something would be.

As Joe cocked his Schofield and leaned out to aim it, his opponent abruptly shifted beneath him. Even as he fired the first shot, and inevitably missed, he realized what the warrior was about. The cunning son of a bitch intended to use his own rope against him. Desperately, he snapped off another shot, but faced with the twin distractions of a dizzying drop and a moving target, that went wide too.

The pain in the wounded man's thigh was almost intolerable, but his rage against the unexpectedly dangerous interloper kept him moving. Even as another bullet flew past him, the Anasazi stretched out to his full extent and seized hold of the line. As it momentarily took his entire weight, the pine tree at the other end of it sagged sharply.

Joe was using the diminutive trunk for support, and the abrupt movement took him completely by surprise. Falling sideways so close to the yawning drop provoked sheer terror in him, and he instinctively reached out with both hands to steady himself. As his frenzied grip closed around the limber pine, the Schofield predictably toppled over the edge. The compensation for its loss was that it struck the straining Indian a painful glancing blow, before plummeting away down the mountainside. That left the white-faced scout with only one remaining firearm still loaded, which unfortunately was also the most cumbersome, but he just didn't have the time to start fumbling in his pockets for more shotgun cartridges.

At the other end of the now taut rope, the Anasazi wiped his bleeding forehead against a raised arm. The falling weapon had nearly achieved what the others hadn't, but the additional source of pain merely concentrated his anger into action. With only one properly functioning leg, the only way he could now reach his opponent was by using the rope. And since the man above would undoubtedly possess a knife, he had to move fast. His well developed arm muscles bulged with effort as he heaved himself aloft.

As the rope began to sway and creak, Joe knew that he really only had one choice. Slicing through it with his Bowie would have been the expected and simplest course, but he also recognized that without its support, he would simply be unable to leave the crevice – the thought of going backwards out into the void was just too awful to contemplate. And so that only left the Winchester. Leaning to his left, he swung the carbine off his shoulder and levered in a cartridge. Then he poked the muzzle over the edge until it was parallel with the rock face, and fired.

The Anasazi saw the 'fire stick' pointing directly at

him, and knew that he had just the one chance. Kicking out with his only good leg, he suddenly found himself almost horizontal, just as the gun discharged. The bullet missed him by a hair's breadth, and then he was on the move again. Maintaining his aspect from the face, he allowed his powerful upper body to take the strain and began to rapidly walk his way up to the crevice. His astonishing speed was driven both by desperation and the burning desire for revenge.

Joe could have cried with frustration. It was as though his opponent possessed some magical protection against hot lead. Frantically he withdrew the Winchester to reload, but even as his throbbing left hand grabbed the fore stock, he suddenly saw a pair of obsidian eyes appear before him. Before he could even react to that shock, a vice-like grip closed around his left ankle, and abruptly he was in imminent danger of being dragged out of his refuge. He literally didn't have time to work the lever action, and so did the only thing left to him.

As his body began to shift down the short slope, Joe hurled the Winchester at his adversary's face, and then drew his Bowie. With one hand holding the rope, the Anasazi had to release his intended death grip to fend off the heavy carbine. That left him momentarily vulnerable, and the white man took his chance. Clinging on to the tree with his right hand, Joe doubled forward and plunged the massive blade into the warrior's belly. He then gave it a savage twist, and watched with relief as his victim's eyes bulged from the overwhelming trauma.

Nothing human could absorb such punishment. As the fingers of his left hand began to loosen on the lifeline, the Indian frenziedly attempted to lock his other hand around it, but the necessary strength had left his body. And yet, even with death imminent, he still managed to gather the wherewithal to propel a stream of spittle towards his killer. Then, quite abruptly and without uttering a sound, he was gone, his stomach sliding off the great knife with a nauseating sucking noise.

Although taken aback by the sheer hatred that had projected the phlegm over his face, Joe nevertheless leaned forward to his limit, so as to observe his deadly foe fall to earth. The corpse, because by then it must have been one, smashed into numerous outcrops before finally coming to rest far, far below. For long moments afterwards, Joe remained transfixed by both his opponent's horrendous demise and the dizzying drop that never failed to horrify him. He found it hard to believe that he had actually bested such a formidable enemy. Then, without even troubling to wipe the spittle from his sweaty features, Joe Eagle released a great sigh of relief, leaned back and closed his eyes.

When he finally came too, he had absolutely no idea how much time had passed – yet passed it had. With a shock, he noticed that the sun was long beyond its zenith. Unless he wanted to spend a solitary night on the mountain, he had to make a move. Groaning with pain and stiffness, Joe briefly glanced over the edge of his refuge and shivered. The thought of attempting the descent filled him with dread. Only the rope's reassuring presence gave him the courage to leave the ledge.

He delayed his departure long enough to reload the twin chambers of his only remaining firearm, and then slung it between his shoulder blades. The broad blade of his Bowie was coated with dried blood, but there could be no help for that. With a grimace of distaste, he sheathed it and then seized hold of the rope. A jolt of pain surged through his left hand, but he would have to get used to that.

'Come on, you lazy bastard,' he muttered, and with his mouth suddenly as dry as rawhide, he twisted around so that his legs were hanging out over the great void. Allowing his upper body to take the strain, he cautiously lowered himself out of the crevice. As his feet found tenuous holds, he paused for a moment, drawing in deep draughts of air to steady his nerves. Terribly aware that the real hard work wouldn't begin until he had exhausted his lifeline, Joe kicked out at the unyielding rock face and began his lonely descent of Pike's Peak.

Even the painful swelling on his lower jaw where Cartwright had punched him couldn't detract from his pleasure at having recovered so many ancient bones. In the time since that great oaf had departed, Othniel Marsh and his three remaining employees had packed up a great many, of all shapes and sizes. And yet, as the sun began to dip towards the western horizon, all four men began to glance nervously at the hillside nearest their position. Mudge had earlier collected together a great deal of wood, which was in place between the expedition and the high ground. That man now glanced over at his employer and uttered a mild rebuke.

'I sure hope Dave didn't take those cross words to heart. We might well need that Winchester of his, come dark.'

Marsh rubbed his chin ruefully. 'It was me came off worst, you know,' he remarked sharply, but was unable to maintain his petulance for long. 'Nevertheless, I hope he'll come back to us.'

The words were barely out of his mouth, when an eerie noise echoed around the hillside. The whole nerve-jangling situation was all too familiar for Ben Mudge, who immediately recognized the sound of a bone horn. Shivering involuntarily, he peered over at the apparently empty hillside for long moments, before coming to a decision.

'I'm going to start a small cooking fire,' he announced. 'We need to eat while it's still light, 'cause come nightfall those devils will likely be down our throats.' He hesitated slightly at the notion of giving further instructions to his boss, but then thought, 'What the hell, everyone else has!'

'Whoever's still alive come daybreak, gets the hell out of here with what we've collected. And that applies whether Dave and Joe make it back or not, because if they ain't here by then, they just ain't coming.'

Marsh's eyes widened with surprise at such author-itative and chillingly prophetic words from his normally reserved collector. But they did serve to cut through his pre-occupied professional enthusiasm, and he recalled with a sudden jolt that of course it was on this very spot that Joe Leidy had met his end. Nodding his head gravely, the scientist offered no protests of any kind.

'Buckskin' Dave eventually made it to the foot of Pike's Peak without having encountered any Anasazis. The reason for that was obvious. As he had predicted, the surviving warriors were doubtless massing for a 'make or break' assault on what remained of the expedition.

He soon located the scout's tethered horse, which whinnied uneasily at his approach. Releasing the nervous creature, he shifted position, dismounted and tethered the two animals together for company. Then, with his Winchester in the crook of his arm, he cautiously prowled on foot around the area where Joe had begun his ascent.

It wasn't long before Cartwright discovered a bru-tally pulverized corpse amongst the rocks. His heart leapt with trepidation, until he realized with relief that unless the scout had taken to wearing animal furs, it couldn't possibly be him. Closer examination of the disgusting mess revealed a large knife wound in its belly, and he grunted with satisfaction, before muttering, 'Dime to a dollar, that was a Bowie knife.'

Peering directly upwards, he stared long and hard

at the mountainside, but the light was already beginning to fail, and he just couldn't make out a human
form. Sighing with disappointment, he then continued to scrutinize his surroundings, and it wasn't long
before he spotted what remained of a Winchester
carbine. 'Hot dang! Everything's falling from the sky
today,' he remarked to the gruesome cadaver.

After that, all he could do was what he was most ill
suited to: settle down and wait to see what developed.
Time passed, and the last of the light began to bleed
out of the sky, but still he maintained his lonely vigil.
Logic dictated that if the only body on the ground
was that of the Indian, then Joe had still to be up
there.

From somewhere nearby came a scuffling noise,
and the hackles went up on the back of his neck.
Easing back the hammer on his carbine, he anxiously
searched his immediate environs. There was a fair
amount of moonlight, but with so many rocks of all
shapes and sizes that also meant an abundance of
shadows to torment the observer. Then, from directly
above and behind, he heard a vivid obscenity that
could only belong to a white man.

'Joe Eagle, is that you?' he called out softly.

There was a moment's silence, followed by, 'That's
a damn fool question. Who the hell else is gonna be
climbing Pike's Peak in the dark?'

After gently lowering the hammer, Cartwright
eagerly scrambled up towards the familiar voice. And
then he saw him – a bloodied, desperately weary
figure on the point of collapse. Quickly he leant his

135

support, and together the two men completed the final few yards to relatively flat ground.

Barely able to comprehend that he had made it, Joe, aided by his very welcome companion, finally allowed his aching legs to buckle beneath him. 'Water,' he gasped. 'And some pemmican wouldn't go amiss.'

After providing him with food and drink, Cartwright gazed in wonder at the exhausted individual for some considerable time, before dropping down next to him. The two men, one lying, the other sitting, remained like that in silence for at least a full hour, with Cartwright keeping watch. Sadly, it was the unmistakeable sound of gunfire that finally put an end to Joe's far too brief respite.

'You able to ride?' Cartwright queried with genuine concern.

Joe nodded slowly. His body felt like hammered shit, but yes, he could ride. There wasn't any other choice. 'Sounds like Mister Marsh has got himself into trouble again,' he remarked huskily.

'Yeah, and as usual it's up to us to get the son of a bitch out of it,' the other man retorted. 'What we have to do for money!' He gestured at the nearby corpse. 'That pus weasel looks like he died hard. What say we take him along to show his *compadres*?'

Despite his fatigue, Joe couldn't restrain a chuckle. 'Might give them pause at that.'

Leaving him to get to his feet in his own time, Cartwright removed a coil of rope from his saddle, and tightly tied one end of it around the Indian's legs. One limb had been splayed out at an extreme angle, indicating a bad fracture, but none of that mattered. 'If he gets tore up much more, there won't be anything left,' he remarked drolly.

Pausing on the way to his own horse, Joe glanced down at his victim. 'If you ask me, he looks too damn good. That climb was the hardest thing I've ever done, an' he near on finished me.'

'Looks like you did a pretty fair job of disarming yourself up there,' the other man responded, as he viewed Joe's empty holster. 'You got any cartridges left for that sawn off?'

'Enough to send a few more of them straight to hell!'

And so, with continued firing coming from the basin, both men mounted up and carefully made their way through the rocks by the light of the moon. Cartwright just couldn't resist one more attempt at humour. 'Try not to misplace any more firearms, huh? Otherwise you'll have to resort to throwing rocks, like the cockchafers we're up against!'

CHAPTER ELEVEN

Nothing much of any real consequence had happened until darkness fell – and by that time, all four men accepted that there would be no sleep for anyone that night. All around the nearby hillside, bone horns were sounding off, accompanied by high-pitched, unintelligible chanting. Bathed in moonlight, dark shapes occasionally flitted amongst the rocks, but they were mostly too vague to waste a cartridge on.

With everyone having eaten his fill, Ben Mudge had expanded the fire to a roaring blaze, but its flickering light didn't reach the high ground. The animals were hobbled well behind the conflagration, with the men spaced out in pairs in front of them, Winchesters at the ready. Marsh and his partner were on the left flank, with the other two on the right, and the fire forming the foremost part of the defensive triangle.

Mudge, who had pretty much taken charge, glanced at the teamster next to him, and at the same time called out to the others: 'Remember, don't let anyone get carried off *alive*. And don't fire together unless you have to. That way you can cover the man who's reloading.' As he spoke, his face was ashen and his eyes intense. It was all like some ghastly repeat of the first time, deliberately set up to torment him for his sins. Although never a religious man, he began to mumble bits of the Lord's Prayer, recalled from his childhood. 'Deliver us from evil, for thine is the kingdom, the power, and the glory . . .'

Othniel Marsh, a man firmly rooted in science, stared over at him for a moment, but held his tongue. If ever a man needed some form of faith, he decided, it was here and now. As if emphasizing that fact, a momentous shriek echoed around the high ground, and suddenly many pairs of feet were in motion.

'They're on the move!' one of the teamsters yelled stridently and very unnecessarily, his nerves getting the better of him.

'Which means we'll finally get to see them, so take a knee and pick your targets,' Mudge commanded, his entreaties to a higher power abruptly forgotten. 'And don't just blast away like frightened amateurs!' Unhappily, that advice was to be swiftly forgotten.

With their mouths dry and hearts thumping, the expedition's beleaguered members reduced their silhouette, and nervously anticipated the onslaught. They didn't have long to wait!

Stone-headed spears arced in towards them, but the range was too extreme and the white men could see them coming. Most fell short or were easily avoided.

'Hold your fire,' Mudge hollered, sounding uncommonly like an army sergeant addressing the ranks.

Then, with a collective howl, a ragged line of paint-daubed Anasazi warriors burst into view on the far side of the bonfire, the moon's rays combined with the flickering firelight endowing them with a nightmarish appearance. Marsh stared in utter horror at the appalling sight. He had never faced anything like this before. Not even the attempt to abduct him could compare, because for most of that incident he had been senseless. Yet he couldn't run away, because he had no idea where to go. So instead he began to fire his carbine like a berserker, discharging cartridge after cartridge without really aiming properly. His obvious fear infected the teamster next to him, who in turn started to fire indiscriminately.

Even so, the range was so short that some of the hot lead, thrown with tremendous power, inexorably tore into the charging warriors, and war cries rapidly turned into cries of pain and distress. The man partnered with Mudge also opened up, and the Indians advance began to falter. With the inferno an impassable barrier, they had no choice but to directly confront the might of the repeating 'fire sticks', and as before, they were receiving a bloody response. But then the inevitable happened. The gunfire slackened off and shortly ceased entirely, as all three carbines needed reloading at the same time!

As his weapon dry fired, Marsh was particularly horrified. His red-rimmed eyes momentarily fastened on to the milling savages, before he began to frantically cram fresh cartridges through the Winchester's loading gate. His fear was enhanced by the Anasazis' renewed howls as, realizing that they were no longer being bloodily picked off, the warriors renewed their charge. Even though unexpectedly lacking a leader, they still possessed enough initiative to press the attack.

Although having given up years before, Ben Mudge had a sudden violent desire for a chaw of tobacco. Instead, he had to merely content himself with angrily sending a stream of phlegm down to the hard ground. Then he stepped forward, levelled his carbine and opened fire for the first time. Not for him the frenzied discharge of lead. His time in company with Cartwright and Eagle had not been wasted, and he worked his weapon with controlled speed, picking his targets. Yet having to alternate between both flanks reduced his effectiveness, and this time the Indians kept coming. A yelling brute came straight for him, and he only just swung the muzzle over in time.

As his gun discharged, his victim was so close that the man received both a bullet *and* powder burns to his skull. Desperately, Mudge worked the under-lever, but their attackers suddenly seemed to be coming from all sides. He swung to his left, firing into a bare midriff, and blood spurted out like a

141

geyser. A huge shape loomed on his right. Frantically levering in another cartridge, he turned to meet it, but just wasn't quick enough.

A massive, curved bone axe slammed down on to his collarbone with sickening force, effectively ending any chance of further resistance. As a tidal wave of pain engulfed him, a great, primeval shriek erupted from his lips, and the Winchester fell from his grip forever. Before Ben Mudge even understood what was happening, his assailant brought the primitive weapon around in a great 360-degree arc and smashed it into the other side of his neck. The field collector's irrevocable destruction was complete.

Othniel Marsh stared in abject horror at Mudge's broken body. At the same time, he was trying to push another cartridge through the loading gate, but it just wouldn't go. 'God damn it, get in, get in,' he snarled. And then it suddenly dawned on him that the magazine must be full. Frantically working the under-lever, he took aim at Mudge's killer and fired.

The bullet struck the Indian full on in his chest, at the same time as one of the teamsters fired at him as well. That second projectile ploughed a bloody course through his neck, bringing him first to his knees and then on his face next to the man he had just hacked to death.

The three survivors were now all reloaded and firing, but the Anasazi had closed the distance, and could sense victory. They well knew that in hand-to-hand combat their superior numbers would give them the advantage. The expedition was about to be overrun, and there wasn't a darn thing its members could do about it!

Realizing this, Marsh chose a shameful course. Turning on his heels, he broke into a run . . . only to trip over one of the very bones that he had come so far to recover. With a cry of dismay, he tumbled painfully to the hard ground, instinctively dropping the Winchester as he tried to break his fall.

The two isolated and now leaderless teamsters kept shooting because there was simply nothing else they could do. Both recognized they had no chance of reaching their horses and making a break for it – all that remained for them was violent death, *or* gruesome and protracted torture. It was this thought that suddenly prompted one of the men to place the hot muzzle under his chin and awkwardly attempt to reach the trigger with his thumb.

The sudden outbreak of violent activity in their rear took the Indians totally by surprise. A brace of horsemen crashed into their midst, and the deeper reports of a shotgun filled the night air. Two warriors were blasted to the ground in rapid succession, and then one of the riders cut through the rope that he had been trailing, and gestured in triumph at his trophy.

'That's right, you heathen bastards,' bellowed Cartwright triumphantly. 'Behold your chief in all his glory!' As though to punctuate that, he opened up with his Winchester and began pouring accurate fire into the suddenly bewildered natives.

Even though taken completely by surprise, it still wasn't the white men's guns, or even their unintelligible words that finally broke the warriors' spirit: it was the sight of their leader, lying almost unrecognizable like a pile of chopped meat, which turned the tide. With their will to fight now utterly shattered, they hoisted their dead ruler aloft and rapidly made for the high ground.

The teamsters, almost unable to comprehend their abrupt turn of fortune, jubilantly sent a few shots after the fleeing men, but their saviours were no longer interested. They'd had enough of killing for one day. Joe simply rode over to the fire, dismounted close to it, and slowly, reflectively, reloaded his shotgun. 'Buckskin' Dave chose to approach his supine employer, involuntarily sprawled amongst a choice selection of the coveted dinosaur bones. Gazing down at him, he just couldn't resist a comment.

'Looks to me like you're as happy as a pig in shit, *Mister* Marsh.'

That dejected individual, knowing full well that he had let down both himself and his men, chose to ignore the remark. He had had more than enough of fieldwork, and desired only to get his precious collection back to Denver and thenceforth on a train to the infinitely more civilized East.

When the new dawn eventually arrived, the eighth since leaving Denver, the five bloodstained survivors peered around at the carnage in silence. The remainder of the night had passed peacefully enough, with neither sight nor sound of the Anasazi, but the trauma was still too raw and occupied all their thoughts. Of them all, only Joe had managed any 'shut-eye', and only then because his exhaustion simply overwhelmed any other factors.

Even the normally ebullient Cartwright was in a subdued mood, yet it was nothing compared to the gloom that had descended on Othniel Marsh. The sight of Ben Mudge's broken body in the harsh light of day had been too hard to take. The fact that the field collector had already survived one traumatic encounter in the basin, only to fall victim on the same spot, seemed particularly cruel. And of course, guilt was a major feature in the scientist's thoughts. The teamsters hadn't actually commented on his cowardice, but the ice in their eyes said it all.

It was some time before anyone moved, but finally someone located the coffee pot and the makings. As the men sat around the remains of the fire, supping coffee and adrift in their own thoughts, Cartwright lit up a cigar. That commonplace occurrence attracted more than casual interest from Joe. 'I'd take it real kindly if you'd save one of those *cee*gars until we're in sight of the rooftops. I might have need of it before then.'

The other man gazed at him curiously. 'I reckon I can do that,' he replied. 'But when we get there I'll want to know the reason why.'

'Fair enough.'

Their employer had barely registered the bewildering exchange. He had other matters on his mind, and a decision to enforce. 'When we depart this accursed place, we're taking Mudge's body with us.'

Cartwright favoured the bloody ruin with a swift glance before responding. He was temperamentally quite unable to leave such a notion unchallenged. 'That's just a piece of foolishness. We're burdened enough as it is with all these God damn bones, without adding to the load.'

Marsh flushed angrily, and for once was not prepared to be dissuaded. 'That man helped to save our lives. I will not simply leave him here to rot, or be skinned as a trophy by those devils. Do I make myself clear?'

Cartwright offered a thin smile. The previous day, those exact same words had been a prelude to a devastating right hook, but such a response was wholly inappropriate now. Instead, he employed logical argument. 'I understand your thinking, boss. I really do. But that stiff will start to turn long before we reach Denver. The stink will be overwhelming, and we'll all be having to breathe in the foul vapours. It just ain't right!'

Marsh agitatedly licked his hairy lips for a long moment, as he pondered the problem. Finally he nodded. 'Very well. I accept what you say. So instead, we will carry him one full day's travel from here and then bury him. And I will say some words over his grave.'

'What if the ground's too hard?' Cartwright doggedly persisted.

Marsh sighed impatiently. 'Well then, we'll build a cairn of stones over him, to keep the animals off. That's the least we can do for him, and the least I'll accept. God knows there's no shortage of rocks. Oh, and if you ever throw a punch at me again, I'll have you arrested. Do I make myself clear?'

It was Cartwright's turn to lick his lips. He knew that he was being baited, but accepted that he kind of deserved it. 'Yeah, yeah, I guess so. And I suppose Mudge does deserve a decent send-off. After all, he was fool enough, or brave enough, to come up here twice, wasn't he?'

Before Marsh could reply, a harsh, humourless voice cut in. 'If you *ladies* have quit gossiping, there's more important things to consider.' Joe Eagle was in no mood for niceties. His damaged hand was tormenting him unmercifully, his face was cut and bruised from the nightmare climb, and the remainder of his body was just one big ache. 'When we clear out today with what you've already collected, I don't reckon we'll have any more trouble with those hostiles. They've got more than enough hurting and dead to handle, and a new leader to choose. But that ain't the end of it.'

The scientist viewed him with frank bewilderment. 'What on earth can you mean?'

Cartwright gave a short laugh, but otherwise stayed out of it. He knew exactly what the scout was about to say.

147

'You don't really think that asshole Cope just high-tailed it empty-handed back to his fancy railroad carriage in Denver, do you? I'd bet my pay *and bonus* from you that he's down there somewhere waiting on us. And in case you hadn't noticed, there ain't as many of us as there once was!'

A sick look came over Marsh's features. He had genuinely forgotten all about his ruthless rival. 'What can we do? Surely there's not to be *more* killing?'

Joe grunted. 'I reckon I might be able to pull a surprise on him. It'll need a bit of preparation, mind. And *you'll* have to completely trust me and go along with it, savvy?'

Marsh's bearded features screwed up into a grimace. 'I don't think I like the sound of this!'

Joe's eyes were suddenly as hard as granite. 'I don't give a damn what you think. All I aim to do is get the rest of us out of this alive.' His expression softened slightly as his glance took in the others. 'And I don't ever want to see Pike's Peak again for as long as I live!'

CHAPTER TWELVE

Brad Dix could scarcely believe his ears. A large number of shod hoofs were approaching his position in Platte Canyon. They were still some way off, but their presence could mean only one thing. And so quite remarkably, after all these mind-numbingly boring days on watch, he actually had something to report. His earlier, apparent reliability had acted as a two-edged sword, because his employer had seemingly decided that he was the ideal man to act as lookout. A more intelligent man might have considered that he was only where he was because Cope had developed doubts about his earlier story.

Having been alone since daybreak, the isolation had again begun to work on Dix's habitually nervous disposition. So now, he didn't even wait around to catch sight of the returning expedition. He just mounted up, and gratefully headed back to the others. Such was his relief at having something to do, it didn't occur to him that the survival of Marsh and his men made a mockery of his earlier, graphic account of their annihilation.

149

'You ain't gonna believe this, boss,' Dix breathlessly
and innocently announced as he finally joined that
man near his tent.

'Surprise me,' came the jaundiced response. A day
or so earlier, Edward Drinker Cope had finally
decided that he was wasting both his time and
money. It was only stubborn pride that had prevented him from returning to Denver with his tail
between his legs.

'It's them. They've only gone and made it back.
Who'd have believed it?' He paused, his eyes eagerly
searching his employer's ruddy features. It was only
then that the implications of what he'd just said
finally struck him, and abruptly his face was a graphic
picture of confused emotions.

Cope immediately understood Dix's dilemma.
Since he wasn't temperamentally suited to forgive-
ness, a wolfish grin quickly spread over his face.

'By *them*, I take it you mean Othniel Marsh and his
minions, supposedly brutally slain days ago by the
savage hordes.'

Dix wasn't sure what 'minions' meant, but he
knew enough to realize that his one hundred dollar
bonus might now be in serious jeopardy. Aware that
his curious companions had sauntered over from the
fire to join them, he possessed enough native
cunning to realize that he needed to emphasize the
positive aspect of his news.

'They're on their way through the canyon right

now, so at least we ain't been wasting our time out here.'

'How many?' Cope barked out.

Dix twitched nervously. 'I don't rightly know. Thought it best to hightail it over here straightaway, so as they wouldn't catch sight of me. I ain't joshing you, boss. It has to be them. From the number of animals on the move, it couldn't rightly be anyone else.'

The other man regarded him with obvious distaste, but had the sense not to let his annoyance sidetrack him. Looking at the others, he commanded, 'Right, you four split up on either side of the canyon entrance. There's to be no shooting unless I say. All I want is the bones.' Briefly returning his attention to Dix, he added, 'You'll stay with me. That way you'll get first look at these ghosts of yours.'

Jared Tiegs couldn't resist a snigger. 'Maybe that's all they are. Maybe he's been asleep all morning, woke up to scratch his ass, and took fright. Or just maybe he's made it all up to get his self a fresh pot of coffee.'

'I ain't saying how's I'm perfect, but none of that's true, and you're a black liar for saying such,' protested Dix, with a pretty fair display of righteous indignation, although he *was* beginning to think it might have been better if the sounds in the canyon *had* been part of a dream.

Tiegs bristled at being called a liar. His hand dropped towards his holstered revolver, but Cope had heard enough. 'Save your anger for whoever's coming through that pass. All of you, get to your positions, and don't do anything until I say.' He glared at the gunhand, until finally that man reluctantly moved off to mount his horse. Nonetheless, there was a rigid set to his shoulders that showed he had retained the anger in his system.

If Cope had had more experience of hired guns, he might have spotted the danger signs. As it was, all he really cared about was a consignment of ancient bones.

Well past the site of the Anasazis' rock fall, and with the end of Platte Canyon nearly in view, Joe Eagle suddenly twisted in his saddle and stared pointedly at 'Buckskin' Dave. 'Reckon it's time for me to sample that last *cee*gar, don't you?'

Marsh sniffed noisily. 'It's a bit early to be celebrating, isn't it?' Even though he'd observed some of Joe's preparations, he still hadn't quite grasped his intentions. Had he done so, he would probably have had a conniption fit.

'Just make the best of it,' Cartwright responded cryptically, as he reluctantly handed over his last 'smoke'. He hadn't noticed anything untoward, and could only presume that the 'Injun' in Joe had sensed something.

As the expedition continued on its way, with the South Platte river flowing companionably on their left, they rounded the last corner, and there before them lay the foothills that would take them back to Denver. A great sigh of relief emanated from Marsh and his teamsters, but the other two just glanced knowingly at each other. Joe ignited one of his precious Lucifers and presented it to the cigar. Under Cartwright's envious gaze, the scout puffed contentedly on it for a moment or two to capture the taste. Then he urged his horse over to the nearest heavily laden mule.

'Bunch 'em up,' he commanded. 'I want all the mules packed as tight as possible around this critter. So they're almost falling over each other.'

'What the hell for,' protested one of the teamsters. 'We're nearly on to open ground.'

'Just do it,' Joe snarled. 'Or I'll kick you so hard you'll be wearing your ass for a hat. An' I ain't on about no four-legged ass!'

The other man frowned, and glanced at his employer, but Marsh merely nodded, before favouring Joe with a curious stare. The knowledge that civilization was now truly within reach, meant that the scientist might have got up the courage to offer a stern rebuke. Then something registered on his peripheral vision and his head jerked around to face the two horsemen who had suddenly come into view.

'Joe?' Marsh called out, his annoyance completely forgotten.

'I see 'em.'

'What do we do?'

'Well, it's pretty obvious what they're after, but it can't hurt to have a parley,' Joe replied. 'You can do the howdy-do's, but follow my lead if things turn sour.'

153

With Joe and Marsh up front, they all continued more slowly until suddenly the canyon walls were no longer there. Unfortunately, they were replaced by a pair of armed men on either flank. Squatting down amongst the stones, they easily had the drop on the mounted party. Affecting to ignore them, the scout instead greeted the two facing him, whom he had immediately recognized as Cope and the thug he had thrown through the railway carriage door.

'How do? Mighty kind of you to throw a welcoming party, but I don't guess it's me you've come all this way to talk to, is it?'

As if confirming that fact, Cope completely ignored him and instead concentrated his attention on his social equal. 'Good afternoon, Othniel. I really must congratulate you. You've triumphed against all odds. It *almost* seems a shame that we have to relieve you of your prize, but then such is life.'

To give him his due, Marsh managed to appear relatively composed as he replied. 'Good afternoon to you, Edward. I have to say that I would have preferred to meet under different circumstances. As it is, I can only demand that you give us the road. I have business elsewhere, and you have no right to obstruct us like this.'

Cope confidently stroked his moustache. 'At the risk of sounding boorish, I would remind you that might is right. And thanks to those heathen savages, we appear to have you outnumbered. We also have the advantage of position, so you really have no choice. Just leave all the pack mules and ride on.'

Joe had heard quite enough. His left hand rested on the bulging saddle-bags of the mule next to him. Cartwright's last cigar was wedged in the corner of his mouth, glowing nicely. Without any warning, he pulled a length of fuse from the bag and seized the 'smoke'. 'If you two *gentlemen* have finished jawboning, *I'll* tell you what's gonna happen. You've probably noticed that all these mules are a mite cramped for space. Well there's a reason for that. Unless you want to be blown to kingdom come along with all your precious bones, you tell those bar trash to stand down and then get out of our damn way.'

Cope's face was abruptly suffused with colour, as he absorbed the outlandish threat. He vividly recalled the sound of the massive explosion in Platte Canyon, all those days earlier, but surely only a madman would consider self-destruction. 'You wouldn't dare!' he barked out. 'Those old bones aren't worth dying for. Certainly not for a man like you. So just hand them over and I guarantee you safe passage. I don't want any violence against my fellow white men.'

In answer, Joe did the unfathomable. He touched the cigar to the fuse, and as sparks began to fly, suddenly displayed the single stick of dynamite to which it was attached. 'Now listen to me, you piece of shit blowhard. These saddle-bags are stuffed full of these thunder sticks. If this lot blows, all that's gonna be left here is a crater. And you know what? I really don't give a damn. These last few days, I've nearly died more times than I can remember, so every day's been

155

a bonus. And all because of these poxy bones. But now that we've got them, I ain't just gonna hand them over to the first windbag that tries to take them. I'd rather die first. Question is, are you prepared to die to take them?' As he spoke, the sparks moved inexorably down towards the high explosive.

Cope's eyes bulged as he peered desperately over at his fellow scientist. 'Surely you're not going to let him do this? He'll kill us all!'

'He ain't got any say in the matter, 'cause he hasn't had any since we left Denver.' Joe retorted. Even as he spoke, he became aware that one of Cope's flankers was beginning to look decidedly trigger-happy.

Over in the rocks, Jared Tiegs' blood was well and truly up. He was still seething from being called a 'black liar', and now had to listen to this half-breed call the tune. So what if the dynamite did explode? He could hunker down behind his boulder in plenty of time. Yet far better to shoot this loudmouth stone dead first, and that way they might all have a chance.

'For pity's sake,' Cope implored, as he stared in abject terror at the lethal red stick, and oblivious to anything else. 'Snuff that fuse out and you can all go on to Denver . . . with the bones. All of them. You have my word on it.'

'He means it, Joe. Put it out, *please*,' Marsh pleaded. Behind them, the teamsters were on the point of fleeing, and even Cartwright suddenly had his carbine muzzle aimed directly at Joe Eagle's back.

With barely half an inch of fuse left, Joe abruptly

announced, 'Fair enough,' and casually tossed the hissing explosive off into the rocks, over to his left. From then on, it was as though everything moved in slow motion. Tiegs was about to trigger his revolver, but froze with shock at the sight of the spinning object, whilst his luckless companion never even saw it coming. Everyone else simply stared in horrified fascination as they waited for the inevitable to happen. Which it did almost instantly!

There was a tremendous crash, and fragments of stone mixed with flesh and bone cascaded into the air. The boulder behind which Tiegs had been standing was abruptly washed with blood. The animals bucked and twisted in an effort to escape from their handlers, and many of them managed it, taking the easier course down into the foothills.

Ignoring all the drama, Joe maintained an iron grip on the skittish mule next to him just long enough to heave the saddle-bags clear. Then, as the beast made a dash for it, he delved into one of them, and pulled out another piece of fuse. With a bleak smile, he ignited it with the cigar, and then urged his horse forwards until he was directly confronting a completely deflated Edward Drinker Cope. Spots of someone else's blood decorated that man's face, as though emphasizing his sudden despondency.

'So what's it to be?' Joe snarled.

'Just go,' Cope weakly responded. 'I never wanted any killing. After all you've been through, I thought you'd just hand the bones over.'

'Not hardly,' the other man retorted through

gritted teeth. 'You come anywhere near us from now on, an' I'll start tossing some more of these around . . . even back in town. You hear?'

The arrogant scientist, his spirit effectively broken by the bloody violence that was far from his natural environment, merely nodded dumbly. He recognized in Joe Eagle a latent brutality that he could never hope to match, nor would even aspire to. And yet that man wasn't quite finished.

Still clinging to the spitting fuse, he glanced briefly at the suddenly very nervous figure of Brad Dix. 'You and me have had a run-in before. So you'd better believe me when I say that if I see you again, I'll kill you. Savvy?'

Dix swallowed hard, and nodded his head like a marionette. Oh, he savvied all right! Grunting dismissively, Joe urged his mount past the two men and followed on after the pell-mell rush of men and animals. As 'Buckskin' Dave came up level with him, the scout remarked, 'I hope you're not still figuring on shooting me in the back, Dave.'

Cartwright stared at him in amazement for a moment, before breaking into a chuckle. 'And I hope you're not figuring on blowing anyone else up,' he countered.

Joe's battered features suddenly displayed a broad grin, and he pulled the small length of hissing fuse out of the saddle-bag. There was absolutely nothing at the end of it. 'Considering that I've just used the last stick, that would be pretty difficult.'

The other man's eyes widened and his chuckle

grew louder. 'Well, I'll be a son of a gun!' he wheezed.

But Joe Eagle hadn't quite finished. 'You know what really ticks me off the most? The fact that in another day or so, I'll have to start calling that bone-collecting prick *Mister* Marsh again!'

Cartwright's laugh could be heard all the way back up to Platte Canyon.